GOIN' FOR IRON

"I figure the only good Injun's a dead one," the young gunslick said.

Sam Two Wolves pushed back his chair and stood up, all in one fluid motion. "You want to try to make this Indian a dead one? Get up and let iron back up your big mouth."

It was all up to the mouthy gunslick now. He had two choices: stand up and drag iron, or turn tail and run. He had been brought up to hate Indians. Brought up to feel he was superior to the red man.

He slowly stood up. "No damn breed talks to me like that," he said, his words coming out hoarsely.

"Then shut my mouth," Sam said calmly. "Let's see if you can."

The self-proclaimed gunfighter cursed Sam and grabbed for his gun, his face shiny with sweat and his eyes wild.

But his .45 never cleared leather as Sam's hand flashed and his .45 roared, belching fire and smoke.

WILLIAM W. JOHNSTONE
BLOOD BOND

DEVIL CREEK CROSSFIRE

ZEBRA BOOKS
KENSINGTON PUBLISHING CORP.

ZEBRA BOOKS

are published by

Kensington Publishing Corp.
475 Park Avenue South
New York, NY 10016

First printing: July, 1992

Printed in the United States of America

Book One

There is nothing so powerful as the truth—and often nothing so strange.

Daniel Webster

Prologue

"You boys got to settle down someday," the elder Bodine told the blood brothers. "You got to put what you seen on that ridge that day behind you."

"We know, Pa," Matt Bodine said, and Sam Two Wolves nodded his head in agreement.

"But it is not yet that time," Sam added.

"Where are you off to this trip, boys?"

"Who knows, Pa?" Matt said.

"You boys is gettin' the reputation of gunslicks," the older man said. "You don't want that rep hung on you."

"I'm afraid it's already there, Father," Sam said, for this man was almost as much a father to him as his blood father. "But we did not seek it out."

"I know you boys didn't. Well, did you tell your ma goodbye and give her a kiss?"

They had. And they both had a big sack of fried chicken hanging from the saddle horns. The elder Bodine stepped back and lifted a hand.

"You boys know where home is. Come back." He turned and walked back into the house. The blood brothers rode slowly out the front gate.

The two young men were as much brothers of the blood as if they had the same mother and father, which they did not. Matt Bodine and Sam August Webster Two Wolves were brothers united by the knife and the fire and the blood bonding of the Cheyenne ritual that made them blood brothers forever.

Sam's father had been a great and highly respected chief of the Cheyenne, his mother a beautiful and highly educated white woman from the East who had fallen in love with the handsome Cheyenne chief and married him, both in the Indian way and the white man's so-called Christian way. Matt had saved Sam's life while both were young boys, and they had become close. Soon Matt was spending as much time in the Cheyenne camp as at his home on the ranch.

The two grew up together, and Matt was adopted into the Cheyenne tribe, thus becoming a Human Being in the eyes of the Cheyenne. Sam's father had been killed during the Battle of the Little Big Horn, after he charged Custer, alone, unarmed except for a coup stick. Matt and Sam had witnessed the slaughter, and had never told anyone about that day . . . but the elder Bodine had guessed. When the brothers rode down from the ridges to stand amid the carnage, it had affected them deeply. They decided to drift for a time, to try and erase the terrible memory of the battle.

Both were moderately wealthy men for the time. Sam's mother had come from a very rich family back East and had left him well-off. Both Matt and Sam owned very profitable cattle and horse ranches.

The brothers were handsome and muscular young men, in excellent physical shape. Both were in their mid-twenties and both had a wild and reckless glint in their eyes. Sam's eyes were black; Matt's were blue. Sam's hair was black; Matt's was dark brown. They were big men for the time, well over six feet, and weighing a good two hundred pounds each. And they were very agile for men their size. They could pass for full brothers, and had, many times. Sam had inherited his mother's white features, with only his cold obsidian eyes—which often sparkled with high humor—giving away his Indian heritage.

When he knew war was coming and that he must fight, Sam's father, Medicine Horse, had ordered his son from their encampment and ordered him to adopt the white man's ways and to forever forget his Cheyenne blood. Medicine Horse made his son repeat the pledge, knowing that even after his death, his son would not disobey his wishes.

Both Matt and Sam wore identical bands around their necks, made up of three multi-colored stones pierced by rawhide.

Both men were highly respected when it came to gunslinging. It was not a title they sought or wanted, but they were called gunfighters, nevertheless. Of the two, Bodine was the swifter, but not by much. He was becoming a legend, although he didn't know it—yet.

9

Sam was not far behind. It was just that Matt had been at it longer.

Matt had killed his first man when he was fourteen, defending his father's ranch against rustlers. The dead man's brothers came after him when he was fifteen and had the misfortune to find him. They were buried that same day. At sixteen, more rustlers came when Matt was night-herding. Two more graves were added. He lived with the Cheyenne during his seventeenth year and then went to work riding shotgun for gold shipments. Four men died trying to rob the shipments. Two more later made the mistake of calling Matt Bodine out into the street. Neither man cleared leather.

While Sam Two Wolves was back East at college (he hated every minute of it, so he claimed), Matt Bodine was a scout for the Army, when they asked him to and providing it was not a campaign to be waged against his adopted people.

Matt saved his money and bought land. His ranch was one of the largest in the state.

Sam Two Wolves was college-educated while Matt had been educated at home by his mother, a trained school teacher. Matt would be considered very well-educated for the time.

The brothers were not yet ready to settle down on their respective ranches. They were young and full of life, and they had a lot of country to see and a lot of life to live before thinking of settling down.

They now drifted into a small town for a drink and supplies. Matt and Sam ended up getting a hell of a lot more than they bargained for.

1

It was not a typical Western town, a fact that both young men picked up on real quick. There were two general stores, both with the same name painted on the front. Two like dress "shoppes," two barber shops, saddle shops, gunsmiths, and so on. Each store was directly across the wide dusty street from the other.

"Have I suddenly developed double-vision?" Sam asked, as they rode slowly down the street, aware of many eyes on them.

"If you have, so have I," Matt replied. "I have seen some strange sights, brother, but I believe this takes the prize."

Both sensed the tension in the air. And both sensed that they had ridden smack into trouble.

"Do you have any idea where we are?" Matt asked.

"Idaho, I think," Sam said. "Does it make any real difference?"

"I guess not." Matt took a second and longer look

up and down the street. "Weird," he muttered. "Let's get our supplies and get gone from here."

"My sentiments, exactly," his blood brother replied. "I don't like the feel of this town."

Two men stepped out of one of the two saloons and stood on the boardwalk, watching the blood brothers. Matt and Sam noticed that the guns of the men were worn low and tied down. A lot of men wore their guns low and tied, and in a dozen other ways for that matter, so that in itself was not unusual. But it was more than the way these two wore their guns that caught the eyes of the brothers. The guns seemed to be a natural part of the men.

"Hired guns," Matt said softly.

"You know them?"

"I know one of them. That's Burl Golden in the black hat. The other one looks familiar, but I just can't place him right off."

"How about a beer?" Sam mused softly, his words just audible over the plop of horses' hooves and the creak of saddle leather.

"That sounds good. Which saloon? You remember the last time we picked a saloon."

Sam chuckled. "Brother, if we didn't constantly stay in trouble, life would be so boring."

They stepped down from their horses and looped the reins around the hitch rail. After they had used their hats to beat the trail dust from their clothing, the brothers looked up and down the street. The fact that they had automatically slipped the hammer thongs from their guns did not escape the eyes of the many loafers who sat in chairs or leaned against

12

support posts on both sides of the street.

The brothers stepped up onto the boardwalk and covered the short distance to the saloon, pushing open the batwings and stepping into the beery-smelling semi-gloom. They stood for a moment, on either side of the batwings, assessing the unusually large crowd for this time of day and letting their eyes adjust to the dimness.

The men in the saloon had fallen silent, everybody staring at the strangers.

"I think they're both Injuns," a man broke the silence, his voice holding a taunting, ugly note.

Matt glanced at Sam and the other smiled. Together, they walked to the long bar. "Beer," Matt said. "For both of us."

The barkeep kept shifting his eyes from Matt to Sam. Both of them did sort of look like Injuns. Sort of. But so did a lot of other men. The barkeep couldn't be sure and didn't want to offend either of these big, rugged-looking hombres. Both of them looked like they'd been across the crick and over the mountains more than once. He finally shrugged his shoulders, drew two mugs of beer, and slid them down to the men.

"Hey, boy," the same loudmouth called. "You with the one gun. Are you a breed, or what?"

Sam took a sip of beer and carefully set the mug back on the scarred-up bar. He sighed, knowing what was coming. But he damn sure wasn't going to let it alone. "Or what," he said.

"Huh?" the loudmouth called.

Matt smiled and sipped his beer. The beer was cool

and felt good after a long dusty day on the trail. Neither of the two young men were trouble-hunters, but neither were they known to back away from it.

"I ain't drinkin' with no damn Injuns," the bigmouth persisted.

"Then leave," Matt told him, his back to the man.

The batwings pushed open, and a man wearing a star on his shirt stepped inside. He looked around, then walked to the bar and stood staring at Matt. "Connors, right?"

"Wrong," Matt told him.

The marshal waited for a few seconds, then said, "Well, if your name isn't Connors, what is it?"

Something in this town was all wrong, and both Sam and Matt could smell it like the odor of a dead skunk. There was too much tension in the air, and it was thick and ugly.

"I'm Matt and this is my brother, Sam."

"I still think that ugly one is a damn stinkin' Injun," the man with the big mouth said.

"You know that gentleman, Marshal?" Sam asked.

"I know him. Why?"

"Then I would suggest that you tell him to shut his face before he finds his mouth separated from it and on the other side of the room."

"He's got a right to an opinion," the marshal replied.

"That he does," Sam agreed evenly. "And so do I."

"What'd you say about me?" The mouth man shoved back his chair and stood up.

Sam turned and faced him. His eyes were hard and dangerous. "I'm half Cheyenne, Mister. Now if you don't like that, you're wearing a gun."

"Hold it!" the marshal raised his voice. "That's enough. You sit down, Eddie. And you boys drink your beer and then leave town."

"No," Matt said softly.

The marshal stiffened. "Cowboy, you can ride with anybody you like. That's your business. But this town is my business. And when I tell you to haul your ashes, you move. Don't play games with me."

Sam stood facing the man with the big mouth. Matt stood facing the bar, his back to the room, the beer mug in his left hand. "I'm not playing games, Marshal. We just came into town to have a beer and stock up on beans and bacon and coffee. When we've done that, we'll leave. And not before."

"I could put you in jail for refusing my orders to leave town."

The man facing Sam was getting angrier by the moment, his face red and his hand by the butt of his gun. "They're both wearin' necklaces, Marshal. That's pure Injun crap. Let's run 'em out of town."

"Settle down, Eddie," the marshal said. "Just settle down. There's something all wrong here. These two are just too calm to suit me. You boys got last names?"

"We're the Smith brothers," Matt said.

"Why couldn't it have been Callahan, or O'Malley, or Frankenhurt?" Sam asked. "Must you always be so unoriginal?"

"My name's Smith," Matt said with an easy grin. "He's Sam Frankenhurt." He gestured toward Sam.

"Couple of damn funny boys," Eddie said. "I'm

15

callin' you out right now, Injun."

"I'm sorry, Eddie," Sam told him. "My dance card is all filled up for this evening."

A couple of the men in the room chuckled.

"Sit down, Eddie!" the marshal shouted. "I mean right now."

Eddie sat, but he wasn't happy about it.

"Who sent for you two?" the marshal asked softly.

"Nobody sent for us. I told you, we're just drifting."

"What are your real names?" The question was asked very low, so no one else in the room could hear.

"Bodine and Two Wolves," Matt whispered.

A nervous tic appeared at the corner of one of the marshal's eyes.

Before he could respond, a man blurted out, "Hell, I know who them boys are. That's Matt Bodine and Sam Two Wolves."

Eddie sighed and placed both hands on the table top.

"I don't give a damn who they are," another said. "I don't like greasy Injuns."

"Shut up, Prince!" the marshal warned him. He cut his eyes back to Matt. "Nobody sent for you?"

"No one. We're just ridin' through. It looks like we picked the wrong town to light."

"I wouldn't suggest staying long," the marshal said drily.

"This Connors you mentioned," Matt said. "Ben Connors?"

"Yes. You know him?"

"I know of him. Gunfighter from over western

16

Kansas way. He's a bad one. Mean clear through. Why would he be coming to . . . what is the name of this town?"

"Carlin-Sutton."

Sam looked at the marshal. "That's a strange name for a town."

"It's a strange town. And getting stranger. You're in the Carlin half now."

Matt blinked. "I beg your pardon?"

"You boys really weren't kidding, were you? You're just drifting."

"That's right."

"Get your beers and come on over to a table with me. Let's talk."

"What are you gonna do about that stinkin' Injun, Marshal?" Prince hollered.

Sam walked over to the man and Prince stood up, ready to draw. Sam never gave him the chance. What he did give him was a combination of lefts and rights to the jaw, mouth, and nose. Prince flattened out on the floor and didn't move.

"That's one way to shut that flappin' trap of his," the bartender said.

"Bring me a beer, George," the marshal called. "And fresh ones for these boys."

"Comin' up, Tom."

Seated at a far table, the marshal said, "The name is Tom Riley."

"Pleased," Sam said. "Would you explain about the Carlin half of this town, Marshal?"

George set three full mugs of beer on the scarred table top and returned to his station.

"Long story," Tom said. "What maps there are of this area show this town as Crossville. It's been here about twelve years. Founded by two men. John Carlin and Bull Sutton. It used to be a nice place to live. Most folks got along well, and there was really very little trouble. Anyways, John and Bull never have got along well with one another. They both own big ranches, and they have big sons and pretty daughters. And they both think they're the cock of the walk. And so do their kids. Bull and John fought the Shoshoni and Bannock and pretty much settled this area. Give them credit for that. Now we got stagecoaches coming in regular, and it was shapin' up to be a right nice place to live and work and raise a family. That is until Daniel Carlin fell in love with Connie Sutton. It has all turned to road apples since then. Now, mind you, neither one of those kids is worth a tinker's damn for anything. It ain't proper to talk about a good woman, but Scarlett ain't no good woman. Not by a long shot. She's as mean as an angry puma and got her a temper and a bad mouth that'd cause any man to duck down and hide his head in shame. Bull has forbid Scarlett to see Johnny, and John has forbid Johnny to see Scarlett. Of course, they see each other every chance they get, which is often. Now Bull had accused John of settin' the whole thing up so's he can get his ranch, and John has accused Bull of the same thing. The kids of both men is eggin' things on 'cause none of them 'ceptin' Daniel Carlin and Connie Sutton has sense enough to come in out of a rainstorm."

"Both sides are hiring gunfighters?" Matt asked.

"You bet. A lot of them."

"Name fighters?"

"Some of them. Ned Kerry, J.B. Adams, Paul Brown, Dick Laurin have signed on with the Flyin' BS."

Sam almost spilled his beer. "The *what?*"

The marshal allowed himself a smile. "That is one hell of a brand, ain't it? Bull Sutton's brand. And he's full of it, too. Henry Rogers, Rod Hansen, Ramblin' Ed Clark, and Bill Lowry is on the Circle JC's payroll. And them's just the known guns. Every manjack on both spreads is now drawin' fightin' wages, and there don't seem to be no end in sight."

"You can add two more to the list," Sam said, looking out the fly-specked window of the saloon to the street. "Simon Green and Peck Hill just rode up."

Tom clenched his hands into fists and quietly did some pretty fancy cussing for a moment.

"I hate to ask this, Marshal," Matt said, "and I hope you don't take it the wrong way, but which side are you on?"

Tom shook his head. "No offense taken, Matt. It's a fair question. I'm sittin' smack in the middle of this mess. No man, or no two men, own a Western town of this size. We have us a mayor and a town council, and they hired me. Only they can fire me. I'm paid to keep the peace in this town. I intend to do just that and to hell with what goes on outside it."

The batwings shoved open, and Simon Green and Peck Hill stomped in. They each wore two guns tied down low. Matt and Sam and the marshal were sitting in the semi-gloom at the far end of the saloon.

They received a glance from the hired guns, but at that distance the faces of the trio were hard to make out. The gunfighters walked to the bar.

"Whiskey with a beer chaser," Simon said, in a voice too loud. "Both of us. And which way to the Flying BS?"

"Now you know, Marshal," Sam muttered low.

"Look there," Matt said, glancing out the nearest window. "Gene Baker and Norm Meeker riding up. It's getting real interesting around here."

"You boys best leave this saloon," George told the pair at the bar. "You're on the wrong side of town. Get on over to the Bull's Den." He had one hand under the bar, out of sight, and both gunslingers knew that in all likelihood, he was gripping a sawed-off shotgun. Some called them Greeners.

"Easy, now, friend," Simon said. "Just hold your water. We didn't know."

"Now you do," George told him.

"For a fact," Peck said.

Gene Baker and Norm Meeker walked in, and the four gunfighters stared at one another for a moment.

"Well, well," Simon broke the short silence. "Look who the tomcat done drug in. Baker and Meeker. I guess you boys signed on with the wrong side again."

"It damn shore ain't the side you're on, Green." Meeker scowled at him. "It never is. You and me, we'll end our quarrel this go around. Now get out of my way."

"I don't think so."

"That's it!" Marshal Riley said, standing up and

20

stepping into the light from the window. His badge glinted brightly. He pointed at the gunslicks. "Take your difficulties outside of town. There will be no trouble in this town. You two," he said to Green and Hill, "take your butts across the street. Right now."

"Why, sure thing, Marshal," Peck said easily and with a smile. "We sure don't want no trouble with the law, now do we, Simon?"

"Oh, absolutely not," Simon added in a mocking tone. The two men grinned at each other and walked out onto the boardwalk, then across the wide street.

Baker and Meeker looked at the marshal, nodded their heads, and walked to the bar. Tom sat back down at the table. Two men were dabbing at Prince's face with wet towels. He was coming around, but slowly. Sam had really blown out his candle with that last punch on the button.

"What ran over me?" Prince mumbled. "A beer wagon?"

"No," one of those attending him said. "That half-breed Injun."

"I think I better make friends with him," Prince said. "I damn sure don't want him for no enemy."

"Marshal," Sam said, confusion in his eyes. "Do you mean that this country is about to explode in a shooting war because of a proposed *wedding?*"

Tom toyed with his beer mug for a moment. He sighed and shook his head. "That's the reason both men give. But this has been simmerin' on the back burner for a long time. The kids seein' each other is just an excuse."

"Lone rider coming in," Matt said.

Baker and Meeker left the bar and walked to the batwings, looking out. "Ben Connors," Baker said. "Somebody is spendin' a lot of money gettin' him in here."

Connors reined up and swung down from the saddle in front of the Bull's Den.

"Seems like a whole lot of people arriving in this town in one day," Matt remarked.

"For a fact," Tom agreed. "And I hope the two I'm sitting with have decided to leave," he said hopefully.

Matt and Sam looked at each other and grinned.

"Oh, hell!" Tom said. "That's what I figured."

"Jesus!" Prince said with a groan. "I feel like I been kicked by a mule."

2

The brothers got a room at the hotel, which was located at the end of the street in a fork of the road, and which had been declared neutral ground by both warring ranchers. That was because of the hotel's dining room. The chef had been brought in from New York City, and his food was praised by all.

Sam stood by the window of the room and looked up the wide street of the split-apart town. "I wonder what the real reason is behind this war? And I wonder why we don't just saddle up and ride away from this silly mess?"

"The real reason is probably a power struggle, and the reason we're staying is because of curiosity. You can't keep your nose out of other folk's business." Matt ducked his head to hide his smile.

"Me?" Sam said, turning from the window on the second floor. "You're the one who is the busybody."

Matt tried his best to look hurt. He couldn't pull it off. "You really want to ride out?"

Sam smiled and shook his head. "No. We've been on the trail for several weeks, and I'd like a few days sleeping in a real bed. Not to mention some time off from your lousy cooking."

"At least I can cook," Matt told him. "You have a tough time getting water to boil." He stretched out on the bed with a sigh. The brothers had taken baths in the tubs behind the barber shop, then had gotten a shave and a haircut while fresh clothing was being brushed and ironed and their trail-worn clothing was sent to the Chinese laundry, run by a pleasant enough fellow named Wo Fong.

"Whatever is going to happen must be close," Sam said, still standing by the open window. "Two more riders coming in, and they look like they've been on the trail for a time."

"Recognize them?"

"One of them does look familiar. The little man."

Matt heaved himself off the bed and took a look. "That's Little Jimmy Dexter. Texas gunhand. He's little but he's mean as a snake. I don't know that other fellow."

Dexter and his partner swung down in front of the Bull's Den and disappeared inside the barroom.

"I'm hungry," Sam said.

"I could use a bite myself."

The words had just left Matt's mouth when a dozen riders and two buggies came into view, racing down the street and kicking up a lot of unnecessary dust, sending people on foot scrambling for the safety of the boardwalks.

"Must be somebody terribly important," Matt said.

"Or somebody who thinks they are," Sam added. "More than likely, the latter."

"Let's go take a look."

At first, the blood brothers thought they were experiencing double-vision. The desk clerk cleared it all up.

"Identical twins," he told him, after smiling at the confused looks on their faces. "Bull Sutton's girls. Willa and Wanda. Don't get in their way, boys. They're pretty as all get out, but both as mean as snakes. And if you repeat that, I'll call you liars."

The twins sashayed across the boardwalk and wiggled into the lobby. One of them spotted Sam and pointed to him. "You there!" she hollered. "Water our teams and see to our buggies and be quick about it."

Sam looked at her, one eyebrow arched. "See to your own buggies," he told her.

"Oh, Lord," the desk clerk muttered. "And this started out to be such a nice afternoon."

The Flying BS riders who had crowded into the lobby stopped in their tracks and slowly turned, facing Matt and Sam, giving them hard looks. The desk clerk quickly dropped on all fours behind the counter.

"Boy, you don't talk to Miss Willa like that," a puncher said. "You better do like you're told and do it quick."

"I don't think so," Sam replied.

"Let's drag him," Wanda said, a wicked look in her eyes. "Somebody get a rope."

"What nice young ladies," Sam muttered.

"Yeah," Matt agreed. "They were at the top of

their class in charm school, for sure."

Several of the Flying BS riders took a step toward the brothers, and Matt and Sam braced for trouble.

"Break it up!" Marshal Tom Riley spoke from the doorway. "Right now."

"Aw, hell, Tom," Willa said, and with those words, the brothers knew she was not a lady. "We were just gonna have some fun with this drifter."

"That drifter is Sam Two Wolves," the marshal quietly informed the crowd. "And that's his blood brother, Matt Bodine, standing to his right. If you people want to see blood all over this lobby, just crowd those two about one inch more and see what happens."

The punchers stood easy, being careful to keep their hands away from their guns. They weren't afraid of the blood brothers—they were all drawing fighting wages and rode for the brand—but they knew well the reputation of Bodine and Two Wolves, and this close in, confined to the lobby of the hotel, the brothers would get lead into a lot of punchers, and Willa and Wanda stood a very good chance of getting hurt or killed.

"Miss Willa asked that breed, or whatever he is, to see to her buggy," a puncher said. "The breed got lippy about it. Bull ain't gonna like that one bit."

"You think anybody who doesn't work for your brand is your servant?" Sam asked. "I have news for you."

Tom stepped between the men. "Well, Shorty, why don't you see to the buggies and then everything will work out?" the marshal suggested.

Shorty looked at Sam, an ugly expression on his ugly face. "We'll meet up again, Breed."

Sam smiled thinly at the man. "Anytime you feel lucky, Shorty. Just anytime at all."

"My daddy will hear of this," Wanda hollered. "You can bet on that."

"The people in the next county over probably heard it," Matt said, recklessness swelling up in him. "A pack of coyotes don't make as much racket as you."

"What?" Wanda shrieked. "What did you call me? Did you hear that man, boys? He called me a coyote. I've never been so insulted."

A big brute of a man stepped into the lobby. The man must have stood at least six-feet-six and carried the weight to go with it. He filled the whole doorway. "What's going on here?" he demanded.

Wanda pointed at Matt. "That saddle bum called me a coyote, Papa!" she bellered, rattling the wheel-spoke lamps overhead.

Bull Sutton cut his eyes to a puncher. "Is that right, Laredo?"

"Well . . . sort of," the man said, shuffling his boots. "But not rightly."

Bull sighed. "Laredo . . ."

"What I said was, she made more noise than a pack of coyotes," Matt explained.

A very small smile creased the big man's lips for an instant, and then was gone. "Well, now, she can do that for a fact," Bull said.

"Daddy!" Wanda hollered. "How can you say things like that in front of trash?" She threw her hands to her face in total mortification.

"Be that the truth," Bull said, "I can't let you insult a daughter of mine."

Matt shrugged his shoulders in total indifference. He stood with his hands by his side. Bull studied the young man. There was a flatness in the rider's eyes that he did not like. Then he realized what that flatness represented. Death. He cut his eyes to Sam. The same flatness and lack of emotion was in his eyes, too.

"That's Matt Bodine and Sam Two Wolves, boss," Laredo said quietly.

The big man's eyes narrowed. He cocked his head to one side and studied Matt, then Sam. His eyes shifted back to Matt. "So you're workin' for the Circle JC, now, huh?"

"Wrong. We're just passing through."

"Uh-huh. Well, you just keep right on passin'."

"Wrong," Sam stuck his mouth into it. His back was stiff with anger, and Matt could see it. And when Sam got mad, the odds were pretty good that somebody was going to get hurt—or dead. "We like it around here. So we think we'll stay for awhile. And that is with or without the permission from your lordship."

"That's the breed who insulted me," Willa hollered.

"Lordship," Bull said softly. He grunted and shook his head at the careless and flippant manner of the two young men. "You boys just stay in trouble, don't you?" He cut his eyes back to Sam. "You don't much look like an Injun."

"I really don't know how to respond to that, so I won't."

"You boys want to work for me?"

"No," they said together.

"I pay top dollar."

"Thanks, but we both own working ranches ourselves," Matt told him.

Bull's eyes narrowed at that. He nodded his head. "So I heard. All right, boys. The hotel is off-limits for trouble. But that's as far as the limits go. Outside, you're on your own."

Matt started to tell the man that they didn't need nursemaids, but wisely decided not to push his luck. Bull Sutton looked like he ate chuck wagons for lunch—wheels, rims, and all. And picked his teeth with the wagon tongue.

"Get your shoppin' done, girls," Bull said, turning his back to the brothers as a way of dismissal. "But stay on my side of the town."

Willa and Wanda looked at the brothers, both went, "Huumph!" and swished out the door, followed by several punchers who acted as body-guards. Bull and several of his men went into the hotel dining room. Matt and Sam stepped out onto the long porch of the hotel.

Matt studied the town for a moment. "This is the craziest thing I've ever seen."

"Well, at least it makes the town look twice as big," Sam said cheerfully, his good mood fast returning.

Matt said, "You want to check out the Bull's Den?"

Sam grinned. "Why not? Might as well make both sides mad at us."

They angled across the dusty street and walked up the boardwalk, on the Flying BS side of the town, tipping their hats to the ladies and howdying the men. The ladies smiled, and the men frowned at them.

"Why are the citizens giving us such dark looks?" Sam questioned, just before they reached the entrance to the Bull's Den.

"They don't know what side we're on, I suppose. You ready for a beer?"

"I'd rather have something to eat. They probably have a free lunch in there."

"And we're probably going to get in a fight once inside. It's better to fight on an empty stomach. I keep telling you that, but you never listen."

"Thanks for reminding me," Sam said drily. "But I'm still hungry."

"I thought Indians could go for days without eating?"

"They do now," Sam popped right back. "After listening to the white man's lies and getting stuck on reservations."

Chuckling, the two men pushed open the batwings and stepped inside the Bull's Den.

Those seated at the tables and lined up along the bar turned and fell silent as the brothers walked in and stood for a moment on either side of the batwings.

"Paul Stewart," Matt muttered, his eyes shifting to a man standing at the long bar. "That's who rode in with Little Jimmy Dexter."

"I recognize him now. The beard fooled me. He

probably grew it as a disguise because he's got warrants out on him."

"No doubt."

The brothers walked to the bar, spurs jingled softly in the silence, and leaned against it. The barkeep made no move to take their orders.

A lunch of meat and cheese and hard boiled eggs had been set up on a table near the far end of the bar. Sam walked over to it and began building a thick sandwich, spreading the mustard liberally on the bread.

"That's for regular customers," the barkeep told him, a sour note to his voice.

"I'm regular," Sam said with a smile. "A little rhubarb now and then sees to that."

The barkeep blinked and Matt laughed. "Two beers, please," he called.

The bartender ignored Matt's order. "Are you makin' light with me?" he asked Sam.

Sam finished building his sandwich, which now weighed about two pounds and was so thick a moose would have trouble getting its mouth around it. He stuck two hard-boiled eggs in his pocket and turned to the bartender. "Light of you? Oh, no. I thought you were inquiring about my health."

"I don't give a damn for your health! And you don't either, comin' in here."

"Hey, Breed," a gunhand called from a table. "Why don't you go on back to the reservation?"

"The general character and disposition of the immediate company would certainly improve dramatically if I did," Sam popped right back.

The gunny pushed back his chair and stood up, his hands by his guns. Pearl-handled, Sam noticed. "I think you just insulted me, Breed."

"Settle down, Chuckie," a man said.

"Settle down, hell!" Chuckie said, his face flushed. "That damn half-breed or whatever he is said something bad about me. I think."

Sam took a bite of his sandwich and chewed. Matt noticed that his brother held the sandwich in his left hand, his right hand close to the butt of his gun. Sam was proficient with either hand, but, as today, normally wore only one gun.

"What's your part in all this, Bodine?" another man called out.

"None, as long as it stays one on one."

"It ain't none of our affair," another said. "We're out of it."

"The bread could be a bit fresher," Sam said, after taking another bite. "But other than that, I have to say it's a pretty good sandwich."

"Damnit, man!" Chuckie hollered. "Will you pay attention to me and stop all that chompin'?"

Sam looked at the man, and Matt knew then that his brother was going to do something foolish. What, he didn't know. But Sam had a tendency to place more value on human life—even an outlaw's life— than Matt. Sometimes. "I seldom pay much attention to the braying of a jackass."

"Chuckie, man, back off!" J. B. Adams urged. "He ain't done you no hurt."

"He's part Injun, and I don't like Injuns." Chuckie made a half turn and faced Sam fully. "I hope you like that sandwich, Breed. 'Cause your belly's about to be full of lead."

"I really doubt it," Sam's words were softly spoken, but carried well to the man. "Why don't you take the advice of your friends and sit down? There is no need for a shooting."

"Sam Two Wolves," Chuckie sneered. "Big shot gunhand. Hell, you're yellow clean through."

The others in the room started watching Matt Bodine. They knew that if trouble started, and it was only a heartbeat away, if any of them took a hand in it, Bodine would fill both hands with iron and start shooting. At this close range, the barroom would be very quickly filled with dead and dying men. Bodine and Sam would take lead, but that wouldn't help those lying dead on the floor, and no one could be sure it wouldn't be them. All in all, it was a very bad situation, especially for Chuckie, for the most experienced gun-handlers knew that Sam Two Wolves was just a shade behind Matt Bodine when it came to skills as a pistolero. To a man, they wished Chuckie would shut his flappin' trap and sit back down.

The batwings pushed open, and Bull Sutton's bulk filled the space. The man quickly sized up the situation and immediately stepped to one side. Several of his hands went with him. He was not going to interfere. Matt read it right when he figured Bull wanted to see Sam in action, wanted to know just what he might be up against should the brothers decide to ride for the Circle JC. He moved to the bar, and Matt noted that for a big man, Bull Sutton was mighty light on his boots. That was something worth bearing in mind.

The barkeep quietly placed a bottle and several glasses in front of Bull.

"I said I wanted a beer," Matt reminded the man.

"Give him a beer," Bull told the barkeep. "Chuck Babb is quick with a short gun, Bodine," Bull whispered.

"He's not quick enough."

"The breed that good?"

"He's that good."

Chuckie cussed Sam for a moment. Then he stood tense, his hands by his guns. Sam laid his half-eaten sandwich on a table and faced the man square, after pulling a hand on the back of a chair. "This doesn't have to be," Sam finally spoke.

"Yeah, Breed," Chuckie replied, his voice hoarse. "It has to be."

Sam arched an eyebrow and waited.

"Are you gonna grab iron?" Chuckie called.

"It's your play," Sam told him, his voice calm. "I never wanted this trouble."

Chuckie began to have doubts. Sam was just too calm and collected. But he made no move to wipe the perspiration from his face. Any more now would be taken as a move toward a gun. He silently cussed the situation. The damn breed was just too sure of himself. He just stood there, waiting, his face showing no emotion at all.

"A hundred dollars on Chuckie," Bull said softly.

"You're on," Matt took the bet.

"Chuckie killed that Utah gunhand, Rodman,

down on the flats," Bull said.

Matt chose not to reply. He'd watched Sam put his left hand on the chair back and wondered what his brother had in mind. Matt lifted his beer mug with his left hand and took a sip, always keeping one eye on the men in the saloon. And the men knew it. Bull had placed both hands on the bar. They all were familiar with the unwritten rules of gunplay.

Chuckie lost his composure and began cussing Sam, the spittle flying from his lips. Sam waited, his face impassive.

"Now!" Chuckie screamed, and grabbed for his guns.

3

Chuckie's first mistake had been in bracing Sam. His second mistake was in reaching for both guns, for that cut his speed down by a half second.

When Chuckie's hands lifted and just before they closed around the butts of his guns, Sam sidestepped and threw the chair. The chair slammed into Chuckie's chest and knocked him backward, his two shots going wild, the booming reports sending men jumping and cussing and hollering and scrambling for the floor and under tables.

Sam leaped across the short space and collided with Chuckie, riding him down to the floor, his fists hammering into the man's face and body.

His face bloody and his eyes wide and wild, Chuckie wrestled Sam away and got to his feet. He tossed Sam to one side and grabbed at a hideout gun behind his belt at the small of his back. A gunhandler, one of his own buddies, tore the gun from him and tossed it to another man.

"Fists, Chuckie," the gunslick told him. "He could have killed you three times over. Now settle it with fists."

"Damn your eyes!" Chuckie told the man.

The hired gun shrugged his shoulders and stepped back. He might hire out his gun, but a man had to have some honor.

Chuckie took a wild swing at Sam, and Sam ducked it, busting Chuckie hard in the gut. The air whooshed out of the man, and Sam hit him twice to the jaw, left and right. Chuckie went down in a sprawl of arms and legs and came up cussing and swinging. Sam backed up and let him come on. He rocked Chuckie's head back with brutal jabs to the mouth and nose. Blood was dripping from the man's nose and mouth, and one eye was discolored and closing.

Chuckie took a wild swing just as Sam was planting his boots. He hit Chuckie flush in the mouth with a left and followed that with a booming right to the side of the jaw. The gunless gunhand went down and didn't move.

Sam looked at the unconscious man for a moment, shook his head in disgust, and then returned to the bar and picked up his half-eaten sandwich. He met the barkeep's eyes. "Beer," he said. "Right now."

The barkeep looked at Sam, new respect in his eyes. Chuckie had not managed to land even one good punch. The barkeep shrugged his shoulders and pulled a brew, sliding the full mug down the bar to Sam.

Bull Sutton counted out one hundred dollars in

gold coin and placed the money in front of Matt.

"Sam didn't draw," Matt said.

"Doesn't matter," Bull said. "It was a good and fair fight, and the breed won. Take the money."

Matt pocketed the coins.

"Your brother's got nerve, Bodine. I hate to see good men get killed needlessly."

Matt started to remind him that he was ever so anxious to see a gunfight, but he held his tongue on that. "Neither of us intend to get killed, Bull."

Bull finished his whiskey and placed the shot glass on the bar. He turned to leave, then paused and looked back at Matt. "No man ever does, Bodine."

The Flying BS crew had left, with Chuckie tied in the saddle. The man was still too addled to ride alone. He was babbling and cussing. "I sure showed that damn Injun," he mouthed.

"Yeah, you sure did," a friend told him. "You showed your butt is what you done."

Sam and Matt went walking. This time, the men of the town were just a bit friendlier when meeting the brothers. But no one was friendly enough to invite them to supper.

They stopped in at one of the two large general stores, both owned by the same man, but on opposite sides of the street.

"Isn't this rather inconvenient?" Sam asked the proprietor.

"Yeah, it is. But if I didn't do it this way, only one of the ranches would do business with me. Then pretty soon neither of them would, and then nobody at all would. There are little ranches all around here that side with one or the other of the big two. Bull and John would spread the word, and I'd soon be out of business. Don't you see?"

Matt and Sam both blinked at that explanation. Matt said, "If . . . yeah, right. We see. Two boxes of .44's, please."

"Which side are you on?"

"Neither one!" Sam said, exasperated with the whole silly thing.

"Then I can't serve you, boys. I just can't risk it. Go across the street to the other store. Maybe my old woman will wait on you."

Matt and Sam looked at each other, shook their heads, and then trooped out of the store and walked across the street to the other general store. Owned by the same man who had just refused to serve them.

"I'm getting fed up to the neck with this," Matt said. The brothers stood on the boardwalk after leaving the second general store. The lady had refused to serve them.

A citizen passing by stopped and took in their disgusted looks. "There's an old trading post up yonder on the river, boys. It's only a few miles out of town. North of here. Right pleasant ride, it is. The trading post is run by a cantankerous old mountain man name of Ladue. Ladue don't kowtow to nobody, and he'll serve anybody."

"That's the best suggestion we've heard so far," Sam said. "Let's go."

Matt nixed that. "In the morning. It's too late now.

40

And something tells me that night isn't the safest time to be riding around in this part of the country."

Sam smiled. "There are occasions when you do make sense, brother."

"Damnest mess I ever did see," Ladue told the brothers the next morning. "Growed-up men actin' like children."

Ladue's place was long and low, was dimly lit, and was packed to overflowing with every conceivable item one might name. And in the rough bar part of the post, you either drank rye whiskey or nothing.

"Sutton and Carlin don't bother me none, though," the old mountain man continued. "I told both of 'em I'd serve whoever I damn well pleased to serve, and if that stuck in their craw, they could just live with it. I also told the pair of 'em that if they tried to throw their weight around and scare off my regular customers, I still got my Sharps that I killed many a warrin' Injun with and not no small number of white men. And I would get lead in both of them. I ain't seen hide nor hair of either of 'em since then."

Matt and Sam both smiled at the man who looked to be about as old as dirt. This was one man who would shoot first and think about the ramifications of it later. Or he might not think about it at all.

"Rye," Matt told him.

"Water for me," Sam was quick to order.

"I come out here in '15, I think it was," Ladue said. "So that would make me about eighty-five, I think. But I don't rightly know. I do know that I got enough teeth left to gnaw on a steak. Ain't been no further east than Saint Louie since then. Don't want to go no further east, neither. Too damn many people." He looked hard at Sam. "You shape up to have some Cheyenne in you, right?"

"Yes. My father was Medicine Horse. My mother was white."

"I knowed Medicine Horse. Slept in many of his camps. He was a fine and honorable man . . . for an Injun. And you know I don't mean no insult by that."

"I know," Sam said with a smile. Sam knew that his father's thinking had been years ahead of most Indian leaders'. Too far reaching for most of the other chiefs. But, in the end, Medicine Horse knew that the Indian ways could be no more and had elected to die in battle.

Ladue looked at Matt. "You been adopted into the Cheyenne tribe, ain't you?"

"Yes."

"I don't know about the breed yonder, but you got the stamp of a gunslick on you, boy."

"My name is Matt Bodine. This is my brother, Sam Two Wolves."

"Well, now," Ladue said with a chuckle. "I remember now. Medicine Horse did marry him a lady from back East. Sure did. Heared of both of you. Things just might be gettin' interestin' 'round here."

"We're not taking sides," Sam told him. "If we had any sense, we'd move on."

"I'll drink to that," Ladue said, refilling their glasses. "This one's on the house." He grinned at

Sam. For a man his age, he did have a respectable set of choppers. "Even the water. Too much of that ain't good for you, son. So why don't you just saddle up and ride on?" He chuckled. "Oh, I know. You're both young and full of it. I was the same way. First time I tangled with a grizzly I began to realize I wasn't immortal."

"You fought a grizzly?" Sam asked. "What happened?"

Matt stifled a groan and hid his grin. He had known a lot of mountain men and knew they could tell some tall tales.

"Well, sir, it was like this. I was afoot, runnin' my traps just off the northern-most curve of the Snake, when the bear popped up sudden-like. He'd been stuffin' hisself with berries, and I disturbed him, I reckon. I clumb up a tree since I was told that a grizzly don't climb trees. Only problem was somebody forgot to tell the bear that. So, whilst I was climbin' down one side, he was climbin' up the other. We met in the middle and I jumped. Damn bear landed right on top of me. Well sir, we clumb to our feet and the fur flew and the snot got flung. I shot him once, and when that didn't even stagger him, I whopped him upside the head with my good rifle and lit a shuck outta there, with that bear hot on my heels. And a griz can cover some ground, too. I got the scars on my be-hind to prove it. He'd swipe, I'd jump and holler, and he'd roar. Finally, I just couldn't run no more. So I stopped and turned around and whupped out my good knife. I faced that bear, all reared up on his hind legs. I told that bear, 'Mister Bear, I ain't got a damn

43

thing agin you, but this here fight's gonna be settled right here and now. You want to leave me alone, I'll leave you alone. If you wanna fight, come on. Well, he come on." Ladue stopped to take a drink of rye. He sighed and wiped his mouth. "That shore was a hell of a fight," Ladue finally said.

"Well . . . what happened?" Sam asked.

"Well, son . . . that griz killed me!"

While Ladue was cackling and coughing and slapping his knee, Sam looked at Matt, a disgusted expression on his face. "I just had to ask, didn't I?"

Stocked up on ammo and a few personal items, which the stores in town had refused to sell them, Sam and Matt decided to spend the day just getting familiar with the country. Both knew they ought to leave; just pack up their few possessions and ride on out. But they were reluctant to do that. Both of them had more than their share of curiosity—plain ol' nosiness, Sam called it—and neither one of them liked to be pushed and crowded as they had been since their arrival.

"So Robin and his hood are off again," Sam said, as the brothers rode through the land.

"Something like that," Matt said.

"And don't ask who is the hood. You are."

Matt smiled. "But a nice one."

"Do you suppose it's gold?" Sam asked.

"I thought of that. I don't reckon so. The more I think about it, and it sure isn't any of our business, maybe it's just two men who don't get along."

"If parents don't want their kids to see one another, why don't they threaten to disown them, or send

44

them away to school back East?" Sam questioned. "This whole thing is stupid. Let's get out of here."

"If we head back to the hotel right now, we can put some miles behind us by sundown."

"Let's do it."

Their minds made up, halfway back to town the brothers were confronted by a dozen riders, all of them riding horses with the Circle JC brand. Matt knew several of the men, and knew them all for hired guns. One of them, Will Jennings, was a two-bit, back-shooting killer.

"Well, well," Jennings said, after the dust had settled. "If it isn't Matt Bodine and his greasy Injun brother."

"On second thought," Sam muttered.

"Yeah," Matt returned the whisper.

The Circle JC riders had fanned out, effectively blocking the road. Trouble was in the air, and both brothers smelled the intangible odor.

"Relax," Will said. "There ain't gonna be no trouble this time unless you boys start it."

"Well, that's nice," Matt replied. "What's your beef with us?"

"You're fence-stragglers," another Circle JC rider said. "If you ain't for us, then you got to be agin us."

"That is not logical," Sam said. "How about if we just don't give a damn one way or the other?"

"Nobody asked you," another rider said. "So why don't you just shut your trap?"

The blood brothers exchanged glances. First the Flying BS crew wanted trouble with them, now the Circle JC boys were on the prod. It didn't make sense.

"Exactly what do you want?" Matt asked the gang. "Both of us are a little confused about that."

"We get orders, we carry them out," a heavy-set and bearded rider said.

Matt was getting mad and so was Sam. "Orders to do what?" Matt asked.

"To run you two out of the country," Jennings said. "Or to kill you if it come to that. And I'll tell you flat out now, I hope it do. I'm lookin' forward to stretchin' you out on the ground, Bodine."

"I wouldn't count on that, Jennings," Matt said. "Not unless you back-shoot me."

Jennings flushed and closed his mouth. It was obvious now to both brothers there would be no trouble this day. They were all too bunched up.

"The question I have to ask," Sam said, "is this: Why do you want us out of the country so badly, when we're not taking sides in this rather silly situation?"

The crew exchanged glances. It was plain to both Matt and Sam that the Circle JC crews didn't know the why of it, just that they were ordered to deliver the message.

"You boys been warned," the bearded man said. "Ride on out of here. If we ever see you again, we'll start shootin'. That's all there is to it. Now, get!" He wheeled his horse and rode away, the others following.

The blood brothers looked at each other for a moment, and then walked their horses over to a shady area and dismounted. They kicked around an old log for snakes and sat down and were silent for a time, each one trying to make some sense out of this totally unexpected new development.

"You ever had any trouble with anyone named John Carlin?" Sam broke the silence.

Matt shook his head, his hat in his hands. "I never even heard of the man until we rode into town."

"Me neither. How about Bull Sutton?"

"The same. And I never heard my dad say anything about either man. So that lets out any personal grudge again our families."

"They all hate Indians," Sam said, then smiled sadly. "But nearly everybody west of the Atlantic and east of the Pacific hates Indians, so that's no answer."

"Not everybody," Matt reminded his blood brother gently.

"Your father respected the Indian way. He allowed us to wander freely on his land and so he was, as far as the Cheyenne anyway, left alone. But he was nearly alone in that feeling. Ancient history, brother. There is right and wrong on both sides."

"Sam, wasn't there a little paper in town?"

"Ummm. Yes. I saw a building with the words *The Express* on it. That might be a starting point. Brother?"

Matt looked at him.

"We've been warned by both factions. And I believe they mean to start shooting if they see us again."

"I know. Sam, you and me, we've never taken water from any man in our lives." Matt stood up and settled his hat on his head. "I don't intend to start now. I don't like being told to clear out of a place with no

47

good reason behind it. We haven't done a damn thing to anybody in this part of the country. Hell, I've never even been in this part of the country before. But, Sam, no more heroics like yesterday in the bar. That was a foolish thing you did with that chair."

"I know it now. But it seemed the right thing to do at the moment. It won't happen again. I think we've landed in the middle of a deadly mystery, brother."

"You always did have a way with words, Sam," Matt said, then laughed.

"Let's go see the editor of *The Express*."

Ralph Masters shook hands with the brothers and waved them to chairs around his cluttered roll-top desk, in the open area that served as his office. "Oh, my, yes. I heard of your arrival within moments after you got here. I also understand that you gentlemen have been ordered out of the country by the powers-that-be."

"News travels fast," Sam remarked. "But you are correct. Why, is what troubles us."

"You're college-educated, Mr. Two Wolves?"

"Yes. To some degree. My mother insisted on it. And the name is Sam."

"How did you know Sam went to college?" Matt asked.

"By his speech. It was a guess." He leaned back in his chair. "What can I do for you gentlemen?"

"Put some light on why both Bull Sutton and John Carlin want us out of this country so bad they'd tell their hands to shoot us on sight."

"Well . . . that's easy. Bull thinks you're working for John, and John thinks you're working for Bull."

Sam leaned forward. "But we've made it perfectly clear to Bull we were just drifting, seeing the country. And if we get a chance, we'll tell John the same thing."

"Oh, that won't do any good," the editor said cheerfully. He waved a hand. "They won't believe you. They'll just shoot you anyway. This whole country is ripe for a major shoot-out. There must be fifty or sixty hired guns hanging around, just waiting to get into action."

Matt shook his head and Sam asked, "Is everybody in this area mentally deranged?"

Ralph laughed. "Well, actually, no. Even though I can see where it might seem that way to a stranger. You gentlemen just rode into a hornet's nest that was already stirred up."

"By a *wedding?*" Matt asked, disbelief in his voice.

"Well, actually, yes."

"You just answered my question," Sam said. "Everybody around here is crazy."

Again, the editor had a good laugh. "Oh, look. Bull and John have hated each other for years. And no one knows why. The two principles can't even tell you the why of it. Bull built a fancy new house. John did the same. Bull imported short-horns to improve his herd. John did the same. Bull bought a fancy new carriage built in Chicago for his wife; John had one built in Paris for his wife. They've been trying to outdo the other for years. Look here." He rummaged around on his desk for a moment and came up with a newspaper. "They've been buying full page ads. I warned them they could be sued, then I realized how silly that sounded." He opened the paper and held it up. "See?"

The ads were full page and facing each other, in very large type. One read: "BULL SUTTON IS A COW-STEALING NO GOOD CROOK." The other read: "JOHN CARLIN IS A HORSE THIEF WANTED IN TEXAS."

"How long has this been going on?" Sam asked.

"The ads? Oh, about three months, I suppose. Sure is making my pockets fat."

"But this is . . . childish," Matt said.

"Of course, it is," the editor agreed. "When it first started, the ads were really good. Now they've just about run out of bad things to say about each other. That I can print, that is." He again rummaged around on his desk and came up with a piece of paper with hand-printed words. "This is what Bull wanted to run last week."

"JOHN CARLIN IS A LOW DOWN DIRTY SON OF A . . . Whoa," Sam said, not reading aloud the last few words.

Ralph held up another sheet of paper. "And this is what John wanted to run."

Matt read aloud. "BULL SUTTON'S MOTHER WAS A . . ." Matt blinked. "Holy cow!"

"Of course, I didn't run either," Ralph said. "Now they're both mad at me, and both have warned me I'd better not run any editorials about them." He smiled. "But I certainly intend to do just that."

"You're setting yourself up to get hurt if you do,"

Sam cautioned the man.

Ralph shrugged his shoulders at that. "I'm a newspaperman, boys. I print what I see and think. You or no one else can stop the shooting now. It's gone too far. The sheriff is fifty miles away, and he isn't interested in whether Sutton or Carlin kill each other or not. He doesn't like either one of them. But I'm afraid some innocent people are going to get caught up in the crossfire and get hurt and killed."

The brothers were silent as they stared at the editor and owner of *The Express*. Sam finally said, "Now will you tell us the real reason behind the hatred and this impending and very stupid war?"

"Honest to God, boys," Ralph said, "I've told you all I know. That's it. It's stupid, all right. Bull and John are like two big strong bulls in a small pasture. One of them has got to go. They just plain hate each other, and I suppose they always will. Well, I've got to put the paper to bed. Look, stop by any time. If you're able, that is," he added, and this time there was no smile on his lips.

Out on the boardwalk, Matt said, "It's stinks, Sam."

"Yes. But it's not our problem."

"It's about to be," Tom Riley said, walking up to them. "Yonder comes a whole gang of Circle JC riders, with Big John himself leadin' the pack."

4

The Circle JC riders wheeled in and fanned out, facing the three men on the boardwalk. John Carlin was not quite the size of Bull Sutton, but close; a bear of a man nonetheless. Matt figured him about six feet, three or four inches and an easy two hundred and thirty pounds, with massive shoulders and arms and a barrel chest. Like Bull, John looked like a man accustomed to getting his own way—one way or the other. As Matt studied the man, he experienced a very strange feeling. It puzzled him. It was an elusive feeling that he could not pin down. He glanced at Sam. His brother stood watching John, an odd expression on his face. So Sam was getting the same feeling as he was.

The same bunch who had braced them on the road into town now rode with John, including Will Jennings, who sat his saddle with a nasty smirk on his face.

John settled his gaze square on Matt. "My men told

you two gunslicks to get clear of this country. Looks like we're gonna have to escort you out of here."

"These two men can stay in this town as long as they like," the marshal bluntly informed the rancher. "They haven't caused any trouble and until they do, you or no one else except me can give them walking papers. And you damn well better understand that, John."

The rancher flushed, shifting his wad of chewing tobacco over to the other side of his mouth. He said, "Seems to me, Tom, that you're gettin' mighty big for your britches."

"They fit me pretty well, Tom. You and Bull are the ones who thinks you're the Lord God Almighty around here. Now these boys don't work for Bull, and they don't work for you. So that leaves them out of this mess. Now as long as they pay their bill at the hotel, and don't cause any trouble, they can stay. I'm not goin' to tell you or this rabid pack of coyotes workin' for you agin. You understand?"

The rancher sat his saddle and stared at the man. "That's strong talk, Tom."

"I meant every word, John. I'm tired of you and Bull usin' this town for a battleground. And I'll tell you something else, the same thing I told Bull yesterday. I wired the sheriff, and he met with the judge, and I'm now a fully commissioned deputy sheriff. That means I have a whole lot more country to ramble around in after people who cause trouble. And I'm going to swear in three new deputies this day. Van Dixon, Nate Perry, and Hank Davis' boy, Parley. I don't want trouble in this county, John.

54

And I damn sure won't tolerate any in this town. You and Bull settle your differences between you like men should. John, you know me. I cleaned up every mining camp and cow town that hired me on. And I'll keep the peace in this town. And if I have to put handcuffs on you and Bull to do it, don't think for one second I won't. Or kill you, if it comes to that."

"He's all mouth, boss," a rider said. "There ain't no guts behind that badge. Just a bunch of hot air. I ain't never seen none of his graveyards. I think I'll kill you, tin star. I think . . ."

Whatever it was he was thinking, it was his last thought. Tom Riley was no fast gun, only slightly better than average, but he was dead accurate. The marshal drew, cocked, and fired, the .45 slug taking the loudmouth just above the nose and blowing out the back of his head. He tumbled backward from the saddle and lay in the dirt.

The sound of Tom cocking the .45 was loud in the sudden silence. John Carlin watched as the marshal shifted the muzzle slightly. The muzzle was now pointed at the rancher's chest.

"He threatened me, John. And you seemed to enjoy the words. You get my message now, John?"

"I get it, Tom," the rancher said, but his eyes were killing cold and flashing with fury. "And I guess I know which side you're on."

Tom's smile was a sad one. "That's sort of funny, John. It's the same thing Bull said."

The new deputies were sworn in, and the marshal

introduced Matt and Sam to the men. Parley Davis was no more than a kid, having just turned eighteen. But in the West, no matter what the age, when a boy strapped on a gun, he became a man. And when he strapped on a star, he became a walking target for a certain element.

But none of the three new deputies had a reckless or careless manner about them, and both Matt and Sam felt the marshal had chosen wisely, probably after giving a lot of thought to the matter.

Van Dixon, a man around fifty, they guessed, walked along with the brothers. "I come into this country back in '40, boys. Back when the only white men were mountain men. There's still a few of them around. Cantankerous old bastards." He smiled. "But they stay up in the mountains and to themselves and come into town maybe twice a year. Mostly they trade with Ladue. A wise man would leave those ol' boys alone. I damn sure do. Those men was born with the bark on."

"You got right in on the last of the trapping, didn't you?" Sam asked.

"Yep. I saw a lot of country, and made friends with the mountain men and the Indians, when either or both would let me. The trouble we have in this country now, boys, is nothin' new. But you asked who started it? Hell, I don't know. I'd put fifty percent on Bull and fifty percent on John. They come in within weeks of each other and took one look and went to cussin'. Some say they used to be friends. Maybe they was. But I never knew them to be.

"Between 'em, they got about fifteen or twenty

kids. Or it seems that many. They do have twelve or thirteen between 'em. Looks like an army coming in. They got two good kids between them. Dan Carlin and Connie Sutton. Polite and mild-mannered and just real nice kids. I think they're about eighteen-nineteen years old. The rest of 'em ain't worth a bucket of slop. I heard you met Wanda and Willa," he said, doing his best to hide a grin. "Well, wait 'til you meet up with Scarlett Sutton. She'll put both of them to shame. Cuss, Lordy, can she cuss. And mean-spirited, too. Mistreats any horse she rides, and I just can't abide that. The way a person treats a horse or a dog tells everything you need to know about their character."

Both Matt and Sam agreed with that.

"John's got twins, too. Pete and Petunia. But that damn Petunia is no flower, believe you me. She's just as mean and ornery as any man, and her brother Pete is about half nuts. He's killed two men that I know of and wounded several more. He's quick with a pistol. Give him that.

"Bull's spread is over yonder way," he waved a hand. "John's outfit is over there. They got range that meets, and they've always squabbled about that. That's where the trouble will more than likely start."

"There just has to be more than personal dislike," Sam insisted.

Dixon shook his head. "I don't think so, boys. I really don't."

"Have the Sutton and Carlin boys ever tied up?" Matt asked.

"Fist fights and one shootin' that left nobody hurt

57

or dead. They were lucky that time."

Van Dixon left the brothers, and Sam asked, "What was behind that last question, Matt?"

"I don't know. Just curious, I suppose."

They sat on a bench in front of the barber shop and watched as more gunhands—most of them would-be gunhands—rode into town. The marshal walked up and sat down on the bench beside them.

"Not a name in the bunch," Matt remarked, disgust in his voice, when the swaggering, slung-low and tied-down crowd had gone into whatever saloon wanted them. "All of them young studs trying to make a name or wanting to prove something."

"What they'll get is killed," Sam said. "I hope they leave us alone."

"And kill or injure a lot of innocent people in the process," Tom said with a frown. "Damn both Sutton and Carlin. Damn them! They could both sit back quiet and live rich as kings if they'd a mind to."

The three men were conscious of the young gunslingers, after being informed that Matt Bodine and Sam Two Wolves were sitting on the bench, all crowding the windows, looking at the gunfighter brothers. Both Matt and Sam hoped they would not be called out into the street. But both knew with this many toughs gathered, that was inevitable.

"I don't believe this thing is about a wedding, Marshal," Matt said. "Me or Sam."

Tom glanced up from the cigarette he was making. "I don't either. But damned if I can figure out what else there is. I've thought until my head hurt and can't come up with anything other than they just don't like each other."

Sam said, "Here comes a couple of the young hotshots. They look to be about eighteen or nineteen. They're heading straight toward us."

"I don't want trouble in this town, boys," Tom warned.

"What are we supposed to do?" Matt asked. "Run away?"

Tom finished rolling his cigarette, licked, and lit before he replied. "Neither of you have done a thing. You're not trouble-hunters, and you've got a right to travel and a right to enjoy the comforts of a town after the trail. Do what you think you have to do."

The two young gunslingers walked even with the bench and stopped. They were in the middle of the street, standing about ten feet apart, legs wide-spread and hands hovering over the butts of their guns. Both of them were very tense.

Before either of them could say a word, Matt called, "Howdy, boys. Is there something we can do for you?"

"You can stand up and face the Wyoming Kid," one called.

"Oh, my," Sam muttered. "The Wyoming Kid. That strains the boundaries of poetic license."

"Wyoming?" Matt said. "I'm from Wyoming. What part of Wyoming are you from?"

"Huh? That don't make no never mind. Stand up and prepare to meet your match and die."

"I don't know that anyone is ever prepared to die. You sort of remind me of James Rybolt. Are you related to him? He's got a spread not too far from my dad's."

59

"My name ain't Rybolt. I'm the Wyoming Kid. Now stand up, Bodine."

"Go on back to the saloon, boy," Tom told him. "I'll have no trouble in this town."

"You shut your mouth, old man," the other would-be gunslick said. "Or face me. I'm Utah Bates."

"Whoa," Sam said. "What's next? New Jersey Jesse?"

Even Tom got the giggles at that. Before ten seconds had passed, all the men were laughing.

"Stop that!" the Wyoming Kid yelled. "I won't have you laughin' at me."

Tom wiped his eyes and waved a hand at the teenagers. "We're not laughing directly at you boys. Now I'm giving you an order, boys. Go on back to the Bull's Den. Right now. I've got three deputies behind you. All armed with Greeners."

"That's the oldest trick in the world," Utah Bates said. "And we ain't a-gonna fall for it."

The sounds of three double sets of hammers being eared back tensed the young gunhandlers stiff as boards.

"I don't run a bluff, lads," Tom told them. "You ever seen a man cut in two with a sawed-off? It isn't a pretty sight."

Before they could respond, a man stepped out of the Bull's Den and called, "Bates! Kid! Come on back in here. The boss said no trouble in town, and he meant it. Now, come on back and cool down."

"Big Dan Parker," Matt whispered. "I didn't see him come into town."

"I didn't either," Tom muttered. "But he's here."

Slowly the two young men relaxed. Bates turned and began walking back to the saloon. The Wyoming Kid paused and called to Matt. "They'll be a day, Bodine. You and me will settle this."

"We have nothing to settle," Matt told him. "Nothing at all."

"Yeah, we do, Bodine."

"What?"

"Who is the best."

"I can tell you that right now," Tom told the young man. "Now get your butt on back to the saloon and keep out of my sight. Move!"

The Wyoming Kid went, but he didn't like it.

Tom said, "You're all right, Matt. You can stay around here as long as you like. You've both been braced in this town and kept your cool when most others wouldn't. Sam, I'm not so sure but what I wouldn't have put lead in Chuckie. You boys don't deserve the reputation that's hung on you." He stood up and walked across the street to confer with his new deputies.

"It's coming, brother," Sam said.

"Without a doubt," Matt agreed. "What's this coming into town?"

Four men, all wearing long dusters, were riding slowly up the street. They reined in and dismounted in front of the Carlin House.

"Dick Yandle," Sam said. "Last I heard of him, he was in New Mexico."

"That's Raul Melendez in the sombrero," Matt said. "And Yok Zapata, the half-Apache wearing the

61

campaign hat."

Matt paused and Sam looked at him. "You know the fourth man?"

"I know him," Matt said softly.

Sam waited. "Well?"

"That's Phillip Bacque."

"You're joking!"

"I wish. Somebody paid a lot of money to get him out of retirement."

"But he runs a highly successful ranch operation up in Canada," Sam said.

"And we have highly profitable ranches in Wyoming," Matt reminded him.

Bacque stepped up on the boardwalk and turned, facing the brothers. He smiled at them and tipped his hat. He called, "Since faster gunfighters seem to have dropped off the face of the earth, I will content myself with killing you, Bodine."

"You want it now?" Matt called.

Bacque laughed. "No, my young duelliste. But soon. Very soon." He walked into the saloon.

"Now, this doesn't make sense," Sam said. "There is no way he could have known we were here. It has to be a case of pure coincidence."

"One I wish had not occurred."

"He's that good?"

"He'll probably get lead in me."

"Now we can't ride out, even if we chose to do so."

"No. People have heard the challenge. If I rode away, I'd have every punk gunhand west of the Mississippi looking for me. Goddamn that Bacque!"

62

Nate Perry, one of the new deputies, walked up. "Who was that fellow who threatened you, Matt?"

"Phillip Bacque. The French–Canadian."

Nate seemed to pale under his tan. "Jesus, man. John Carlin is really going all out, ain't he?"

"That would appear to be the case."

Sam took a notepad from his inside vest pocket and added four more names to the tally. "That brings it to thirteen known gunhands for Bull and twelve for John. Twelve or fifteen would-be's for each side."

"All because two ranchers don't want their kids seeing each other."

The sounds of wagons, buggies, and horses' hooves pounding the hard-packed roadway reached them.

"More surprises, I suppose," Sam said.

"I do love a parade," Matt replied, as the riders came racing into town amid a cloud of dust and wheeled in at the general store on the Carlin side of town.

"I guess now we get to meet the Carlin kids," Matt said, taking off his hat and attempting to fan the drifting dust away from him.

One of the riders let out a wild Texas yell and jumped down from his horse.

"Bob Coody," Sam said. "You remember him?"

"I remember him. He's walking this way, too."

The Texas gunhand came stomping up the boardwalk and stopped in front of Matt and Sam, grinning down at them. "I heard you boys was here. I couldn't believe it. Last time I seen you boys you was

63

stickin' your noses into matters down along the Pecos. That didn't concern you and neither does this affair."

"What's the matter, Bob?" Sam asked. "Did Josiah Finch run you out of Texas?"

Coody's grin vanished. "Don't nobody ever run me out of nowhere, Breed."

"Get out of my way, Coody," Matt told him. "You're blocking the sunlight."

"If the boss hadn't a said no trouble in this town, Bodine, I'd ask you to make me move."

"Oh, Coody," Matt said, disgust in his voice. "Will you people—on both sides—stop playing kid's games? What the hell is going on around here?"

Bob Coody squatted down on the boardwalk and took off his hat, wiping his forehead with the back of his hand. "Tell you the truth, Bodine, damned if I know. Now, I don't like you or the breed here, and I figure you and me will shoot it out one of these days, but this situation here? It's odd, Bodine. Mighty queer, it is."

"Both sides paying top wages?" Sam asked.

"Best I ever collected. And I ain't fired a shot in a month, 'ceptin' at a rattler the other day. It's borin'."

"We're not on either side, Bob," Matt told him. "We're out of this war."

"That ain't no good place to be, Bodine," the gunhandler told him. "Straddlin' the fence is as good as takin' the wrong side. You better pick one and stay with it. Or get the hell gone from here. Them's my feelin's about it."

"Thanks for leveling with us," Sam said.

64

Coody stood up and hitched at his gunbelt. "This is a strange sichiation here. Gives me a right uneasy feelin' not knowin' which way the wind is a blowin'." He turned abruptly and walked away, heading for the Carlin House.

"Now what do you make of that?" Sam asked.

Before Matt could reply, the air was split by wild curses, followed by gunfire. A man staggered out of the Bull's Den and fell in a bloody heap in the dirt.

5

Matt and Sam remained seated on the bench as the saloons emptied and gunhands lined the boardwalks, staring at each other across the street. Tom Riley came at a run to stand over the still conscious chest-shot man in the dirt.

"Damn spy for John Carlin," a puncher said, the pistol still in his hand. "He drew down on me, and I got witnesses to prove it."

"He's a liar," the dying man gasped the words. "I ride for the A.T. outfit. I just come into town for a drink. I ain't no gunfighter."

The gunslick flushed and said, "You don't call me no liar, saddletramp." He cocked the pistol and shot the dying man in the face.

Tom Riley laid a cosh against the gunslick's forehead, and the murderer went down, a swelling knot right between and just above his eyes. "Nate!" Tom called.

"Here, Tom," the deputy said, stepping forward.

"Get some boys and drag him to the jail. Log him in for murder."

"You'll not get away with this, Tom," a BS rider said. "Bull will not see no man of his on the gallows."

Tom ignored that. "Van, Parley, take down the names of all these men who witnessed the shooting in the saloon. After that's done, you boys ride back to the Flyin' BS and stay the hell there." He turned his back to them and faced the Carlin House. "You men clear out. Right now. Get the hell to the JC range and cool down."

"You murderin' scum!" a woman yelled from the Carlin side of town. "Goddamn trash, all of you!"

Sam and Matt stared at the woman. Maybe twenty-one or so, and definitely cute. But with a voice that would put a steam whistle to shame.

"Petunia Carlin," a shopkeeper spoke from the door of his business. "She's just getting wound up."

The young woman then started letting the invectives fly, shouting the curses across the street.

"My word!" Sam said.

"I told you," the shopkeeper said.

"Petunia!" Tom Riley yelled. "Close that nasty mouth of yours and get on back into the dress shop. Move, girl!"

Petunia stared at the marshal, stamped her little foot in anger, then gave Tom a very obscene gesture. She stomped back into the shop.

A young man stepped away from the crowd and yelled, "You don't talk to my sister like that, Riley!"

"Pete Carlin," the shopkeeper said. "Petunia's twin brother. Crazy mean."

"Why are you talking to us?" Matt asked, twisting on the bench to look at the man. "No one else in town will."

"Shut up, Pete!" Tom told the young man. "Before your butt overloads your mouth."

"Aw, I figure you boys is all right," the shopkeeper said. "You just rode into a bad situation and don't have the good sense to ride out." He turned and walked back into the shop.

"There is some truth in his words," Sam said.

"You don't tell me what to do either, Tom," Pete yelled. "My pa will skin you and nail your hide to the barn door."

Petunia stuck her bonneted head out of the dress shop. "Pete! Shut your damn mouth and get off the boardwalk. You know what Pa said. Move."

Pete muttered something and stepped back into the Carlin House.

The body of the dead A.T. puncher was toted off, and the BS rider was dragged off to jail. Matt and Sam had not left the bench during the entire episode. Tom walked slowly over to them.

"That gunny who squatted down and talked to you boys, who is he?"

"Bob Coody," Matt told him. "From Texas way. He doesn't like me very much."

"Why?"

"He claims I killed a friend of his down along the Pecos."

"Did you?"

Matt shrugged. "It's a possibility."

"The lid is going to blow off this boilin' pot now," Tom said, removing his hat and wiping first his forehead and then the inside band with a handkerchief. "I expect to see the whole kit-and-caboodle of them come stormin' in."

"Petunia appears to be a very nice young lady," Sam said with a straight face.

Tom looked at him, astonished. Then he smiled. "Yes. Oh, my, yes. Very feminine. And what you saw today was only the tip of the iceberg, so to speak. Not that I've ever seen an iceberg. You boys really are stayin' out of this mess, aren't you?"

"We would have backed you if anybody had made a move," Sam told him.

"I appreciate that. See you boys."

The brothers sat and watched the BS and most of the JC riders leave town, galloping their horses and yelling. Pete and Petunia and a few of their hands remained. Matt and Sam sat and watched Petunia and her brother meet on the boardwalk and start up toward the hotel. They were going to pass right by the brothers.

"You know any of the hands with them?" Sam asked.

"Not a one. I think they're regular punchers, but just remember they ride for the brand."

When the brother and sister and entourage got within hearing distance, Pete and Petunia started whispering and giggling and pointing at Matt and Sam.

"Lars," Petunia said. "Do something about re-

70

moving that greasy Injun from my sight, will you?"

"It'll be my pleasure, Miss Petunia," Lars said.

"Here we go," Sam spoke softly.

Lars swaggered up and said, "On your feet, Injun. Get off the street so's decent women can pass."

"I'm very comfortable right where I am," Sam said, and then kicked him right in the nuts with the point of a boot. Lars sank to his knees, his face drained of color, his mouth working open and closed without a sound coming out. Sam put a boot on the man's chest and shoved him off the boardwalk. He landed with a plop and a small cloud of dust.

"You may safely pass by, Miss Petunia," Sam said. "I assure you, this Indian has never molested a white woman nor taken a scalp in his life."

"Ooohhhh," Lars moaned.

"You trash!" Petunia hissed at Sam.

"This foul-mouthed wench is calling me trash," Sam said to Matt. "Since you're my brother, I guess that tars you with the same brush."

"Foul-mouthed wench!" Pete yelled. "Git up on your feet, Injun, and take your lickin' like a white man. Dave, Batty, watch Bodine."

Sam slowly stood up and then uncorked a right that knocked Pete clean off the boardwalk and into the street. Matt left the bench in a rush and slugged Dave hard, knocking the puncher back into Batty. Batty fell off the high boardwalk and landed in a horse trough, his head banging against the side of the trough. He sat there, addled, water up to his neck, and with a stupid smile on his face.

"Why you son of a . . ." Dave never got to finish it.

Matt plowed in, both fists swinging. One punch caught Dave on the nose, and the other slammed into his jaw. Matt followed in quickly, with a left to the wind and an uppercut that clicked Dave's teeth together and crossed his eyes. Matt measured the man and busted him square on the side of the jaw. Dave wilted to the boardwalk.

Sam had punched Pete silly. The young man stood swaying in the swirling dust of the street, blood leaking from his nose and mouth and from a cut on his cheek. Matt checked Lars. Lars was in no shape to do anything except moan.

"Finish him," Matt said. "Quit playin' around, Sam."

"He's got a head like a rock!" Sam said. "He won't go down."

Pete chose that time to smack Sam in the mouth and knock him sprawling on his butt. Matt laughed and applauded. His laugh was cut off short as Batty climbed out of the horse trough and slopped over to him and hit him on the back of the head with a work-hardened fist. Matt went to his knees and shook his head to clear the birdies from it.

Matt rolled and came up to his boots, facing the big and angry puncher. "I'm gonna tear your meathouse down, Bodine," Batty said.

A large crowd had gathered, encircling the fighters. Even Tom Riley was there with his deputies. They seemed to be enjoying the show.

"Knock his teeth down his damn throat, Sam!" a man yelled.

"Who said that?" Pete shouted, looking around him.

Sam decked him, and the young man landed hard on his butt.

Batty swung, Matt ducked, and drove his right fist just as hard as he could into the puncher's belly. Batty doubled over, gasping for air, and Matt hit him with a left that caught the man directly on the ear. Batty staggered to one side in time to catch a punch on the other ear. Batty was in a temporary world of silence, except for the roaring in his head.

"What happened?" he questioned.

Matt gave him a reply in the form of a fist to the mouth. Batty's feet flew out from under him, and he hit the street and didn't move.

Sam had literally beaten Pete's face into a pulp, and still he wouldn't go down. Sam finally spun him around, grabbed the young man by the shirt collar and the seat of his britches and drove him headfirst into a hitchrail post. Pete sighed and sank to the ground, his head resting momentarily on a fresh pile of horse shit. His face slowly sank out of sight.

"Hold that pose!" Ralph Masters hollered, running up with all his cumbersome camera gear.

Sam and Matt leaned against a hitch rail and panted while Ralph got several pictures of the scene, laughing and chuckling all the while.

Petunia stood on the boardwalk, her face white with anger and shock. Nobody did this to a Carlin. Nobody. Ever. Not and get away with it.

"You sons of bitches!" Petunia squalled, just as

Lars was sticking his head over the rim of the boardwalk. Petunia reached into her purse and hauled out a short-barreled hogleg. She jacked the hammer back just as the crowd began running in all directions.

Her finger slipped off the hammer, and she blew Lars' hat off his head. Lars fainted with a prayer on his lips, sure he was mortally wounded.

Matt and Sam crawled under the high boardwalk just as Petunia started letting the lead fly. Her mother had probably stood by her husband's side, helping John fight off Indians and outlaws in the early days, but Petunia was no hand with a pistol. She shot out one window of the general store, fractured the striped pole outside the barber shop, blew the saddle horn off of a hitched horse on the other side of the street, sending the frightened animal racing up the road, drilled a wooden Indian outside the tobacco and gun shop right between the eyes, and sent the sixth shot rocketing toward space.

Dave was just getting to his feet when Petunia hurled the empty gun in frustration. The pistol caught the back of his head and sent him sprawling back into the street, out cold.

Tom and his deputies rushed out from cover, and he told a lady to grab Petunia before she could get her hands on another gun. The ample lady grabbed the girl, and Petunia tore away and socked her on the jaw. The lady rared back and gave Petunia double what she had received. Petunia went down on her bustle with a busted lip and commenced to squalling at the top of her lungs.

Tom ran over and not-too-gently jerked Petunia up and marched her toward the jail. "Thank you, Mrs. Jackson," he said to the lady.

"You're sure welcome, Tom. It was worth a bruised jaw."

Petunia stuck out her tongue at the woman and cussed her.

"Pitiful," Mrs. Jackson said, as Tom marched the young woman up the boardwalk.

"Where the hell do you think you're taking me, you jackass?" Petunia bellered.

"To jail, Petunia," Tom informed her. "And you'd best shut that big mouth of yours before I forget that you're a female and turn you over my knee, take off my belt, and give you what your daddy should have given you years back."

"Unhand me, you brute!"

Van and Nate were dragging the unconscious Pete Carlin up the center of the street. Ralph Masters was working frantically, taking pictures of the event.

Lars opened his eyes and gingerly felt his head. "Am I dead?" he asked.

"No," Parley told him. "Just under arrest."

"That ain't good, but it's better than dead," Lars replied.

And a lone figure slipped out the back of the Carlin House, made his way to the livery, and lit a shuck for home range. John Carlin was going to hit the ceiling when he learned of this.

Matt and Sam crawled out from under the high boardwalk. Both of them were somewhat the worse for wear. "Brother," Sam said, "I know that pride prevents us from doing this, but I honestly think the best thing we could do is saddle up and get the hell gone from this place."

"I agree," Matt replied, brushing the dirt from his jeans and shirt front. "With both statements."

"Goddamn you!" the voice of Petunia drifted out from the jail. "My daddy'll burn this two-bit town to the ground for this."

"Can you imagine being married to that tuba-mouth?" Sam asked.

"I'd sooner bed down with a skunk. Come on, let's get cleaned up and get something to eat. I figure in about two hours, or less, this town is going to have one angry father stomping around."

John Carlin rode into town in force, with every man he could muster, all of them heavily armed, riding with rifles across the saddle horn. It was a formidable army. Carlin's face was dark with fury. Marshal Tom Riley stood alone in front of the jail. He had a spare six-shooter tucked behind his gun belt and held a Greener in the crook of his left arm. His deputies were on the rooftops, armed with rifles. Matt and Sam lounged near the jail. Sam had taken his spare pistol out of his saddlebags and shoved it behind his belt.

"You got my daughter in your goddamn jail, Tom," Carlin said, walking his horse to the boardwalk where Tom Riley stood. "I want her out, now."

"I don't take orders from you, John," the marshal

76

said calmly. "The judge will have to decide what bond will be. There are some serious charges against her."

John Carlin stared at the man. "I hope you're joking, Tom," he finally said.

Tom shook his head. "Incitin' a riot. Resistin' arrest. Disturbin' the peace. Battery upon a private citizen. Assault and battery upon an officer of the law. Destruction of private property. Endangerin' the public safety. The list goes on and on. She stays where she is."

"Tom, I'm here to get my daughter out of that jail. Right now."

"Don't push me, John. I'm warnin' you. I've been pushed all I'm gonna be."

"How about my son, Pete?"

"Pete I can release."

"You're makin' a bad mistake, Tom Riley."

"You want your boy or not?"

John smiled, a tight little brief curving of the lips, and turned his horse, riding over to the Carlin House. He waved for his men to follow him.

Matt and Sam walked over to the marshal. "You think he's stupid enough to try and bust his kids out?" Matt asked.

"Stupid, no. Mad and arrogant, yes."

"Daddy!" Petunia squalled, her voice rattling the windows of the office in front of the jail.

"Get us out of here, Pa!" Pete hollered.

John turned and stared back at Tom. "You've been warned," he said, then walked into the saloon.

"What about those charges?" Sam asked. "Will the

judge uphold them?"

"Some of them. He'll dismiss the others. I just think it'll do the girl good to cool her heels in the jail for a couple of days. Might teach her some humility."

"But you doubt it," Sam said.

"Yeah," the marshal said, a weary note in his voice. "This whole situation is goin' to end in tragedy. I feel it. The kids of both men have been free to do whatever they choose all their lives. Nothin' is goin' to change them now. They don't know no other way of life, and if I read them right, and I think I do, they wouldn't change even if they could."

"Tom," Matt said, "was any of the Carlin kids in that bunch that rode in?"

The marshal gave him a sharp look. "Now that you mention it, no. And that worries me."

"You want us to take the back of the jail?" Sam asked.

Tom looked at them both. "You're dealin' in?"

"Looks like it," Matt told him.

"Step in the office, boys. I'll swear you in as temporary county deputies. I got the power to do that."

"Here we go again," Sam muttered.

"Well, don't complain about it. It was your idea!"

6

Only the three regular deputies were informed of Matt and Sam being deputized. Both brothers took down Greeners from the gun rack and stuffed extra shells in their pockets. They slipped out the back of the jail and took up positions on opposite sides of the building. Their patience paid off after a silent hour. They heard just the faintest rustle of footsteps slipping up the dark alley. Then the shadowy forms of four people could be seen. A fifth man stepped out, then a sixth. Whispers came to the brothers.

"The three deputies is on the rooftops. Tom Riley is sittin' outside the office." Something flashed in the night. "Marcel will be settin' the fire in five minutes. That ought to draw Tom away."

"And if it don't?" someone asked.

"Then we kill him."

Matt lifted his Greener and fired both barrels into the soft night air. The sound was enormous, and it put the six men flat on the ground and brought Tom on a run through the narrow valley. He appeared on Sam's side of the building.

"Get down!" Sam told him. Ten seconds later he had brought the marshal up to date, speaking in a whisper.

"What's goin' on back yonder?" Van called from a rooftop.

"Watch out for a fire!" Matt yelled, reloading the twin barrels of the sawed-off. "Marcel Carlin will be lighting one any second. Alert the fire brigade."

"You men on the ground," Tom called. "And we can see all of you. Stand up with your hands over your head, or we start blasting in ten seconds. I'm counting. One . . ."

"Don't shoot, Tom!" a voice called. "We're standin' up."

"The hell we are!" a defiant voice yelled. The speaker opened up with a .45.

Two shotguns and a rifle barked and boomed at the flashes. The man was blown to bloody ribbons.

"Jesus God!" a voice that Tom recognized as belonging to Clement Carlin yelled. "Don't shoot no more. Stand up, boys. Keep your hands away from your guns."

"I got this little turd Marcel!" a man called. "He was about to set my shop on fire."

The town had thrown monetary reasons to the wind and united at the threat of armed takeover and fire. Men and women appeared with rifles and shotguns and pistols.

"Blast anyone who tries to leave the Carlin House," Tom called. "By the front or the back."

"Will do, Tom," the tobacco and gun shop owner called. "I'll take the back."

The five members of the break-out team were marched up the alley and to the jail. A blanket was tossed over the bloody remains of the defiant one.

Johnny and Clement Carlin and three hands stood sullen-faced in the office. Marcel was shoved inside by an angry citizen. Another citizen carried a jug of kerosene and a bag of kerosene-soaked rags. Marcel reeked of the flammable liquid.

Tom pulled young Parley to one side. "Ride for the judge, Parley. Bring him up to date and escort him back here tomorrow. I 'spect the sheriff will come along, too. Go, boy."

Tom jammed the Carlin brothers and the hands into one cell. He was mad to the core, and his face showed it. "Van, you and Nate stay here." He turned to Matt and Sam. "You boys game for enterin' the Carlin House?"

"Let's go," Matt said.

The three men, armed with sawed-off shotguns, walked across the street, and Tom shoved open the batwings and stepped inside, Matt to his left and Sam to his right. Tom's Greener was pointed straight at John Carlin's belly. Tom walked to the rancher and placed the twin muzzles against his shirt, belly high.

"It's over, John. I don't care what you and Bull do to each other—outside of this town. But if all your hands haven't dropped their gunbelts to the floor in ten seconds, I swear I'll blow your goddamn guts out your back." He cocked both hammers of the Greener.

John Carlin's face was greasy-pale. He knew Tom

81

Riley meant every word he'd said. "Do it, boys," the rancher said. "Right now."

Matt was holding his Greener on the gang at the bar, and Sam was covering those seated at nearby tables. The hired hands and gunnies knew that at this short distance those terrible Greeners would wipe out half the room, and those left alive would be horribly crippled. These were ten gauge sawed-offs, loaded with ball bearings, rusty nails, and God alone knew what else. Gunbelts started hitting the floor.

"All of you," Tom ordered. "Up against that north wall and keep your hands in sight. When all the guns are gathered, you boys can ride out, five at a time. If you show your faces back in this town until after the hearing, I'll kill you on sight. And I think you boys know that I mean every word of that."

The hands and hired guns nodded their heads. They all knew Tom Riley's reputation.

Tom cut his eyes to the barkeep. "George, gather up all those guns and stack them on the bar."

"Yes, sir, Tom. Right now."

Not a word was spoken as George quickly gathered up the guns and placed them on the bar.

When that was done, Tom said, "None of you boys better be holding back a hide-out gun with plans to use it."

"I got a derringer in my back pocket, Marshal," Rambling Ed Clark said. "But I ain't got no plans to reach for it."

"Me, too," Jack Norman said. "But it's gonna stay where it is."

A half a dozen others had hide-out guns, but all

stated that openly and none had plans to try any gunplay. Yok Zapata and Phillip Bacque stood with new respect for the marshal in their eyes. As did most of the hired guns. This, they knew, was a man with no back-up in him and tough clear through. And with Matt Bodine and Sam Two Wolves now wearing badges, this was a team that would be hard to beat. At this moment.

"Startin' with the first five nearest the door," Tom said. "Get on your horses and ride. I'll let you know when you can pick up your guns. Move!"

The saloon emptied quickly. Tom still stood with the Greener shoved up against the belly of John Carlin. "The judge will be here tomorrow, John," Tom told him. "I wouldn't try to keep you away from your kids' hearin'. And you can bring some hands in with you. The way you and Bull feel about each other, I wouldn't ask you to commit suicide by comin' in alone. But all guns will be checked at my office. Clear?"

"Clear enough."

"Git."

John Carlin got.

At the Flying BS, Bull Sutton was awakened from a sound sleep with the news of what had taken place in town that night. He sat in his den and chuckled at the news. Along with nearly everyone in the area, he was sure the judge would do little else but fine the Carlin kids, but the public humiliation would be something they would not tolerate for very long.

John and family would strike back at the town, and they would strike back hard. All Bull had to do was keep his people in line, and John would destroy himself. He and his family would attend the hearings and all have a good chuckle and some belly-laughs at the expense of the Carlins. That would really put the icing on the cake.

All in all, Bull thought, things were working out right well.

Petunia got things off to a rousing start at nine o'clock the next morning by calling the judge "a bald-headed, frog-eyed, son of a bitch."

"Thirty days in jail for contempt of court!" the judge hollered.

Then she told him to go commit an unnatural act upon himself, but not in those words. John's mouth dropped open in shock.

"Petunia!" he shouted.

The judge pointed his gavel at John. "John," he said, an ominous tone to his voice, "far be it from me to tell another man how to raise his children, but this young lady is sadly lacking in social graces."

Petunia started to let the judge have it again, and her mother stuck a handkerchief in her daughter's mouth, grabbed her by the hair of the head, jerked her around, and spoke in low tones to her for a moment.

Petunia never said another word the rest of the proceedings. She sat very still and very pale-faced.

Not even John had a clue as to what his wife might have said to her daughter, but he knew best of all that

Ginny Carlin could be an iron lady when the situation demanded it.

Bull Sutton, his sons, and his crew rode in and stood outside the empty building where court was being held and snickered and giggled. John Carlin's face grew redder as his temper rose with each snicker behind his back.

The upshot of it was that Petunia was fined a hundred dollars and so was her brother—Petunia being released into her mother's custody—and they were ordered to pay the damages for any property that might have been damaged or destroyed. He fined Lars, Dave, and Batty ten dollars. In a separate matter, the judge ordered the BS hand to be taken back to the county seat for later trial on murder charges.

He banged his gavel and court was over.

As soon as the gavel sounded, Bull Sutton bellered, "Well, John, those snooty kids of yours finally got some comeuppance, hey? It's about damn time."

John Carlin walked out onto the boardwalk and knocked Big Bull Sutton flat on his butt in the dirt.

Bull got to his feet and shook his head. "No gunplay," he told his crew. "No matter who wins, no gunplay. This is between John and me."

Then he turned around, stepped up on the boardwalk, and knocked John clear through the window of the packed make-shift courtroom.

"Don't try to stop them," Tom Riley told Matt, Sam, and his other deputies. "That would be like trying to stop two grizzlies with a stick."

"Maybe they'll get it out of their system this way?"

Sam said.

"Or do the town a favor and just kill each other," Tom suggested.

Bull stepped through the shattered space where the big show window used to be and came back out the same space a hell of a lot faster than he entered. John had been waiting for him and gave him a right fist to the mouth that smashed his lips and bloodied the entire lower half of his face.

John jumped out of the ruined window and tried to kick Bull. Bull rolled away and caught John's ankle and jerked, spilling the man to the ground. On their knees in the dirt, the two men fought each other like crazed beasts. Ginny had taken Petunia home in the buggy. Once there, she had plans for a buggy whip and Petunia's backside. Ginny did think she was better than most other people, but she did not approve of her girls using vulgar language . . . at least in public.

John and Bull slugged it out in the dirt. They were wringing wet with sweat and splattered with blood. Their noses were broken and pouring blood. Blood dripped from smashed lips and cut faces. Still neither man would go down for the count. They fought until they were arm weary and exhausted. Bull shoved John away from him and staggered to a hitchrail, leaning against it and catching his breath. John leaned against a wagon, his chest heaving from exertion.

Then the two men looked at each other and each one spat on the ground. Bull cussed John and John cussed Bull. That went on for a couple of minutes.

Laredo got a bucket of water and poured it over Bull's head, and Luke got a bucket of water and dumped it on John. Then the two men went at it again.

Bull would knock John down, and then John would knock Bull down. Each man hit the ground so many times people lost count. Some in the crowd even got bored and went home or to a saloon. Now it was taking the men most of a minute to get off the ground. Both of them were staggering from exhaustion. Both men's eyes were nearly swollen shut. Their faces were puffy and bruised. Still they fought on.

They both swung at the same time and both weakly tossed missed punches, sending the two wealthy ranchers sprawling face-down in the churned up dirt. Neither had the strength to get up, much less continue the fight.

"Load 'em in wagons and get 'em out of here," Tom said.

Sam consulted his watch. "Forty minutes," he said. "Those two dinosaurs fought for forty minutes."

"Too bad they didn't kill each other," Tom said shortly.

The sons of both men gave him dark and dirty looks which the marshal ignored.

"Maybe this settled it," Matt said.

"Don't count on it," Tom replied.

That week's edition of *The Express* carried full

stories of Petunia and her brother and of the big fight between John and Bull. Photographs of both—including the one that caught them sprawled near unconsciousness in the street—could be seen in the windows of the newspaper office. Pictures of Pete Carlin's head in a fresh horse pile was one of the favorites. Petunia's wild shooting was also a hit that brought many smiles. Ralph ran off extra copies of *The Express* and mailed them all over the territory, including a copy to the governor and the President of the United States. For a week, nothing happened and even Tom began to wistfully think that things just might have been settled between the two powerful ranchers and the area would settle down and everybody could live in peace. But he didn't really believe it. He knew both men too well to believe in fairy tales. Not one gunhand from either side rode into town. Young Parley heard that Ginny Carlin took a buggy whip to Petunia's backside, and Petunia was still being real careful about sitting down.

Matt and Sam had just about made up their minds to pull out. It looked like to both of them that with the fight, Bull and John had settled their differences. Neither had won, but then neither had lost.

Matt and Sam were sitting in the marshal's office when a lone rider reined in and stepped up on the boardwalk. "Frank Anderson," Tom said. "Rides for Bull. He's a cowboy. Period. Never had a moment's trouble out of him."

"He's packed to ride," Sam noted. "His saddlebags are full, and his war bag is tied to the horn."

Frank stepped into the office and took off his hat. "Just thought I'd stop and say adios, Tom. I'm haulin' my ashes."

"What's the matter, Frank?"

"Little Jimmy Dexter and Peck Hill are about an hour behind me. Bull is sendin' them in to brace Bodine, there."

"Why?" Matt asked, surprise on his face. Sam was as surprised as his brother.

Frank shrugged his shoulders. "No particular reason, I reckon. Other than just to keep things stirred up. I can't take no more of it. Laredo is the only hand left out there that's worth a damn. All the real punchers have pulled out one by one. I figured I was the only real drover left. I got me a job down in Utah, doin' what I do best, and that's lookin' at the ass-end of cows."

Frank nodded his head at the marshal, and said to Bodine, "Good luck." Then he rode out.

"This makes no sense," Tom broke the silence. "They must know that you two are no longer deputized, and that you have never taken sides against either rancher. Why single you out, Bodine?"

Bodine shrugged and checked each pistol, loading up the chamber usually kept empty under the hammer. "None of this has made any sense to me. Not from the very first. But I won't run, and if they call me out, I'd feel obliged to meet them."

"We will meet them," Sam corrected, as he also loaded his pistol full. He stood up. "I'm going back to the hotel for my second gun. Be back in a minute."

"You boys could ride out," Tom suggested.

"That's not an option," Matt told him. "And there is no law in this territory that says a man can't protect himself. Not yet anyway. Was I you, Tom, I'd clear the streets." Matt stepped out of the office and pulled his hat brim lower, shading his eyes. He waited.

The blood-bonded brothers were waiting on the boardwalk of the now deserted street when the riders came into view. Four of them.

Sam grunted. "I recognize Dexter and Hill. I don't know the other two."

"Local toughs," Tom Riley spoke from the open door of his office. "Les King and Willie Durham. Thugs. They'll do anything for a dollar."

"Well, Tom," Matt said without looking around, "you be sure and bury their dollars with them."

7

Now it all came down to what many called the way of the West. People back in the settled East, with police officers and plenty of courts and judges, abhorred the unwritten code of what they called the savage West. But in the West, if a man sold you three thousand head of cattle, the buyer didn't count them. It was done on the seller's word. And if a man wore a gun and was called out into the street, he went, or in the minds of many, wore the brand of coward for the rest of his life. Honor was everything. Without honor, few folks would trust or do business with a person called coward. Most of those who subscribed to the code would tell you it wasn't right. But it was there, and for as long as it existed, it would be the way of the West.

The brothers watched the gunhands rein up and dismount and walk into the Bull's Den for a shot or two of amber-colored courage.

The brothers rolled cigarettes and waited.

Nothing moved on the wide and rutted street. No chickens pecked the ground, no dogs lay tranquil in the warm sun, and only the four horses of the gunslicks were tied to hitchrails.

"No point in trying to get you boys to back out of this, is there?" Tom asked.

"Nope," Matt replied.

"You know better than to even ask," Sam added.

"I reckon," Tom said. The brothers heard the door close behind them.

"The street isn't deserted," Matt said. "Look up by the newspaper office."

Ralph Masters was hurrying up the boardwalk, carrying his bulky photographic equipment.

"Ralph!" Sam called, pointing. "Set up in that alley and stay out of the line of fire. Don't get killed or hurt for a damn picture."

"I'm a reporter," Ralph countered. "I go where the news is."

The batwings suddenly slammed open, and the Wyoming Kid stepped out.

"Where in the hell did he come from?" Matt questioned.

"He must have come in the back way. Remember we've seen them do that."

"I wonder where Utah Bates is."

"Isn't five enough? You want an even six?"

"I like round numbers."

"Well, you are about to get your liking, brother. Here they come and the sixth is Utah Bates. Stupid punk."

"I hope you don't think we're going to stand out in

the street and face six men, Sam."

Sam smiled. "We stand right where we are until after the first volley. Then I drop down behind that water trough, and you duck into the alley. How's that sound?"

"You're so sneaky, Sam. Is that the Cheyenne coming out in you?"

"Indians aren't sneaky. We're just courageous. Why you do think the white man calls us Braves?"

Both Matt and Sam laughed, and the laughter seemed to grate on the nerves of the approaching gunmen. "What the hell are you two gigglin' about?" Peck called.

"A private joke," Sam told him. "Why are you after us?"

"Why not?" was his reply.

"That makes about as much sense as any of this," Matt whispered.

"And maybe 'cause you is you, and we is us," the Wyoming Kid said.

Sam's mouth dropped open, and Matt said, "Don't even attempt a reply. It isn't worth the effort."

The six men moved closer, all spread out.

"You boys are brave, aren't you?" Matt called. "Six to two. I guess they really are scared of us, Sam." And with that said, Matt drew his right hand .44 and took out Little Jimmy Dexter, the slug catching the evil little gunman in the stomach and doubling him over.

Sam was only a split second behind Matt, and he ended the career of Peck Hill just as the man was clearing leather, his slug striking the tall hired gun directly in the center of the chest and exploding the heart. Hill stretched out on the street and kissed the earth.

Sam jumped for the protection of the trough, and Matt beat it for the alley just as Ralph Master's flash pan popped. The Wyoming Kid spun around, both hands filled with .45s, and started firing at the reporter. He saw his mistake too late. Just as the Kid tried to turn, Sam leveled a .44 and dusted the Kid, from right side to left. The Kid toppled over in the blood-stained street, hollering for his mother.

Watching from the window, but down on his knees behind the wall for protection, were the marshal and his deputies. Tom said, "He should have listened to his mother ten years back. It's a little late now."

The remaining three toughs had seen the error of the open street, and while their friends were going down, they were high-tailing it to cover. When one of their shots went wild and shattered a window in the marshal's office, the code of the West went flying out the same busted window. Tom grabbed up a Winchester and went out the back door, circling around and coming up the same alley where Ralph Masters had set up his equipment and was flash-panning away.

"You damn fool!" Tom shouted at him. "Are you tryin' to get killed?"

"Just doing my job, Tom," the editor called over the rattle of gunfire. "This is great stuff. The folks back East will eat it up."

A wild shot tore off a chunk of board just over his

head and ricocheted off, whining down the alley. The newspaperman yelped and dropped to his knees.

"Good," Tom said. "Now stay there." He crouched at the edge of the building, looking the situation over. Tom took a deep breath and yelled, "You Flyin' BS riders. This is Tom Riley. Give this up, right now."

His reply was several bullets that thudded into the building. Tom leveled his Winchester and gave as much as he received, working the lever as fast as he could, his fire pinning down the punk who called himself Utah Bates.

Utah jumped through a window and landed on the floor of the dressing room of Miss Charlotte's Fashionable Gowns, a curtain around his head and neck. A young lady who had been in the process of changing clothes stood before him, clad only in the scantiest of underthings. She let out a wail that would have given a cougar heart failure just as Miss Charlotte came around the corner, a shotgun in her hands. Utah Bates scrambled to his boots and went back out the same window he had entered just as the shotgun roared. Several pellets caught him in the ass, and he bellered out his pain, hit the ground, and crawled under the building next to the dress shop. A dog had just given birth to a fine and healthy litter of puppies under the building, and she was in no mood to be trifled with. Utah and the dog came face to snout in the cool semi-gloom. Seemed to Utah this dog had enough teeth for two. Utah yelped, the dog barked, and the protective new mother bit Utah on the nose, and he went rolling and hollering out the back of the building, bleeding from the snoot and the butt.

Les King broke and ran, leaving his buddy, Willie, to fend for himself. Willie quickly assessed the situation and found it not to his liking. The hired tough hit the air and headed for the country. He could always steal a horse.

Matt and Sam and the marshal stepped out into the street, reloading as they walked. The Wyoming Kid was still moaning in pain and calling for his mother.

Dr. Blaine came running, carrying his little black bag, and the undertaker was two steps behind him.

"Get after those others!" Tom yelled to his deputies. "Bring them back here. And I don't give a damn whether they're sittin' a saddle or tied acrost it."

The brothers and the marshal stood over The Wyoming Kid. The doctor looked up at them. "He might live, but I doubt it. All depends on what the slug destroyed as it passed through."

"To hell with him," Little Jimmy Dexter cried out. "What about me?"

Doc Blaine checked him quickly. "You're finished, man. Make your peace with God."

"You go to hell, sawbones," Dexter gasped.

"Now, now," the undertaker soothed. "You can be assured that you will be stretched out fine." He thought about that. "How fine depends on whether or not you got any money. You got any money on you?"

"Git your nasty hands offen me, you leech!"

Dexter told the man.

"Ungrateful wretch!" the portly mortician said.

"You," Tom Riley said, pointing to a citizen. "Go get their horses and take them to the livery. They now belong to the town and all their possessions with them."

"Well, now," the undertaker beamed. "I suppose you will have a nice service after all."

"Bastard!" Little Jimmy Dexter gasped. He cut his eyes to Matt. "You're quick, man. And sneaky, too. I like that. You're all right, Bodine. I'm glad it was you who done me in."

"I'm not," Matt said quietly.

"Born to the gun," the small man said. "Both of you. No matter what you do, you'll never get shut of the smell of gunsmoke."

"We can try," Sam said.

"Won't do you no good. You're just like Hickock and Longley and Masterson and the Earps. So long, boys." Dexter closed his eyes and died.

Matt noticed that the man's clothing was frayed and patched, and his boots were worn out. He took a double eagle from his vest pocket and handed it to the owner of the general store. "Get him a new suit for burying." He and Sam turned as one and headed for the hotel.

"Strange man," the shopkeeper remarked.

"No," Tom said. "He's just good with a gun, but not a killer. There is a world of difference 'tween the two."

*   *   *

The Wyoming Kid lay leaning toward death in the doctor's small clinic, unaware of the quick burial of Little Jimmy Dexter and Peck Hill. Willie Durham, Utah Bates, and Les King had beat it back to the Flying BS range and safety.

The sheriff rode down from the county seat and said he couldn't see any charges that might be brought against the men. It was a simple case of men calling out other men. There was no law against it. He admitted that it didn't make any sense, but added that since when did Bull Sutton or John Carlin do anything that made any sense?

Tom Riley certainly had to agree with that.

As far as Matt Bodine and Sam Two Wolves were concerned, they felt free to pull out and were packing up to do so when Sam noticed an envelope someone had slid under the door. Sam picked it up and opened it, removing a single sheet of paper. Someone had printed, "CHECK THEIR BACKTRAIL."

"Check whose backtrail?" Matt asked.

"Sutton and Carlin, I suppose. Why ask us to do it? Why have we become the central players in this mystery? What business is it of ours?"

"Let's go see Tom."

Tom studied the words on the paper for a long time. "No idea who slipped this under your door?"

"No," Matt said. "We didn't hear a thing."

"Who would know about Sutton and Carlin?" Sam asked.

"Ladue," Tom said quickly. "He's older than dirt and was here before anybody else."

"I'll wager Ladue didn't slip the note under our

door," Sam said. "Someone in this town did that."

"Who and why?" Tom asked.

Both brothers shrugged, Matt saying, "That's a mystery to us, too."

"I don't like mysteries," Tom said, leaning back in his chair. "They irritate me. Someone in town either knows something about Sutton and Carlin, or they want us to think they do. If it's the latter, why?"

"To throw us off the real trail," Sam said. "But I tend to think they don't know as much as they suspect something might be down their backtrail."

Tom pointed a finger at him. "You'd make a good lawman." He paused. "If you boys were to stick around, the county would pick up your hotel tab. But not your food," he was quick to add. "You two eat like lumberjacks."

"You want us to go see Ladue?" Matt asked.

"If you would."

"You boys totin' badges?" the old mountain man asked.

"In a manner of speaking," Sam replied. "If you know what I mean."

"You is and you ain't," the man said. "Sure. You're hepin' out Tom Riley. Tom's a good man. And he don't kowtow to nobody." Ladue studied the pair for a few seconds. "You wanna know about Carlin and Sutton. Well, pour some coffee and park your butts, and let's get to jawin'."

They sat around a rough table, and Ladue slowly spoke. "There was somethin' odd about them two. I

sensed it right off. Bad blood between 'em right off
the mark. They come in here with their wives and
their kids and a bunch of no-count men a-trailin'
cattle with the brands reworked so sloppy a one-eyed
drunk could have seen it a week away. And them two
wasn't a month apart gittin' here. It was like it
was . . . well, planned. But the way they feel about
each other, you know it wasn't. It was just one of
those things, I reckon. But . . . give 'em credit for a
few things howsomever. They fought Injuns and
outlaws and so forth and settled this area. They done
that, all right."

He took a sip of whiskey and said, "I think they
come in from Missouri. Both of 'em. But they wasn't
Missouri borned. I disremember the cowboy's name
who told me that. Not that it makes any difference,
'cause shortly after he did, he was found shot stone
dead. Him and me we got on right good—the
cowboy, I'm talkin' about—and he said . . . Kain-
tucky! By God. That's where he said Carlin and
Sutton come from original. Sure did. 'Bout fifty mile
from one another back yonder. I asked if Carlin and
Sutton knowed each other back there, and he said he
didn't think so."

"Did they ever socialize?" Matt asked.

Ladue shook his head. "Not to my knowledge.
And that seemed odd to me. You see, other than the
few mountain men who stayed in this area, them two
was the first whites to come in and settle. But I don't
never recall them gettin' together for no funnin'."

"Not even the women?" Sam asked.

"No. And the kids hate each other. 'Ceptin' for

Daniel Carlin and Connie Sutton."

"What happened to make the kids hate each other?"

Again, Ladue shrugged. "I guess the parents taught them to hate. Hell, 'ceptin' for Connie and Dan, all them kids is as squirrely as a tree full of nuts. And the girls is just as unpredictable and dangerous as the boys. The boys has all killed. Ever' one of them. they like to kill. You can see it in their eyes. Mean, rattlesnake eyes. Rabid coyote eyes. You both have seen the type. And there ain't nothin' wrong in their heads neither. They're just mean. Bullies. They like to hurt people and animals, and I ain't got no use for none of them. I told Johnny Carlin to his face that if I ever caught him on my property, I'd kill him on sight with no words needed to be spoken. They all leave me alone. One of these days, the Carlin kids and the Sutton kids is gonna meet up somewheres, and they's gonna be the God-awfulest shoot-out this territory's ever known. You just mark my words on that."

"What you've told us today," Sam said. "Have you ever told anyone else?"

Ladue shook his shaggy head. "No. No reason to. Nobody ever asked me."

8

The brothers talked with the old mountain man most of the afternoon. Before they left, Sam told Ladue he should write all this down; it was a part of history.

Ladue had smiled. "I've started to a dozen times, lad. But who would believe it? You should have seen this country when I come out here. It was the most beautiful sight I've ever seen. Injuns, now, they respect the land. White man, he just takes from it and don't make no effort to put back. Seems like white men, they got to dig and gouge and cut and clear, and they don't look no further than the end of their noses. White men, it seems, don't respect nothin' 'cept money and power. White man is greedy. They always want more than they need."

"That old man makes a lot of sense," Sam said, as the brothers rode slowly back to town. They were off the road and keeping to a game trail. Both of them felt that was safer.

Before Matt could reply, they heard the sounds of

horses on the road below them and reined up. They dismounted, holding the muzzles of their mounts and whispering to the horses, in an effort to keep them quiet.

"I don't care what you say," a man's voice drifted up to them, over the slow prod of horses' hooves. "This deal don't make no sense, and I'm pullin' out. Me and Junior is headin' down to Utah. I'm gonna tell you something, Ben, Bull Sutton is crazy as a road lizard and so is John Carlin. And them kids of theirs is nuttier still. Hold up here, I think I got a loose shoe."

There was a moment of silence, then the flare of a match to a cigarette. "It ain't clear to me," the voice came out of the near dusk. "If it was cattlemen agin sheepherders or nesters, I could see it. Cattlemen fightin' over water rights, fine. That's clear. But why are these two spreads fightin'? Lord, man, they got everything in the world and more. It ain't water, it ain't land, it ain't sheep, it ain't nothin' that I can see. Two kids wanna get hitched up. So big deal. I ain't dyin' over no damn weddin'."

"There's more to it than that," Ben Connors said.

"Then you tell me what it is?"

"I don't rightly know," Ben admitted.

"See? You don't know either."

"I know the pay is good. Best I've seen in a time. I ain't turnin' my back on that much money."

"Ben, I ain't got nothin' agin Matt Bodine and Sam Two Wolves. I ain't afraid of 'em, but I ain't got nothin' agin them. Why does both Sutton and Carlin want Matt dead? Him and Sam just drifted in and was plannin' on driftin' out. This deal is crazy!"

"I'm aimin' on killin' Bodine 'cause I want to kill him," Ben said.

"Not if I can call him out first," a third man spoke up.

"He's faster than you, Big Dan," Ben said. "And faster than you, too, Dick. You boys leave him to me."

Ben Connors, Dick Laurin, Big Dan Parker, and a couple of others who had not yet been identified. Sam and Matt cut their eyes at each other. Each one knew what the other was thinking: It just keeps getting weirder and weirder.

"That shoe loose?" the rider was asked.

"Naw. I pried out a stone. He's all right. You ready, Junior?"

"Let's ride."

"See you, boys," the man said. And two horses cantered away from the group.

"I never figured Henry for yeller," one of the group said.

"He ain't yellow," Dick said. "Him and Junior just might be the onliest ones with any sense amongst us."

The men rode on. The brothers waited until they could no longer hear the sounds of the hooves before they chanced uttering a sound.

"Sam, I am beginning to get PO'd about this," Matt said, some heat in his voice.

"Understandable."

"I feel like calling Bull and John out. Both of them. Together."

"Not a good move, my brother. As big as Bull is, you'd have to hit a vital organ or a big bone to even jar him. He'd get lead in you. Besides, this mystery is becoming intriguing. Don't you think so?"

Matt gave him a dark look and swung into the saddle.

"Where are we going?" Sam called.

"To see Bull Sutton."

"Have you taken leave of your senses?" Sam shouted.

"No," Matt called over his shoulder. "Are you coming or not?"

Muttering and shaking his head, Sam took out after his blood brother. He was thinking some perfectly terrible things about Matt Bodine.

"Hallo the house!" Matt yelled, from a respectable distance from the huge two-story home.

"Boss!" a hand called, disbelief in his voice. "It's that damn Matt Bodine and Sam Two Wolves."

"What?" the brothers could hear Bull's beller even from where they sat their horses.

"Let me kill him, Pa!" a Sutton whelp shouted.

"Shut up!" Bull shouted. In a lower tone of voice, he said, "Let them ride on in, Clet. Pass the word, no shooting. They didn't come here to make trouble. They're brave boys, but not stupid."

Matt and Sam rode up to the big mansion and swung down from the saddle, looping the reins around a metal ring set in a hitchpost.

Bull Sutton faced them from the large porch.

"Come on up, boys," he told them. "The only people who have ever been turned away from a meal at this house was named Carlin. Mother, tell the cook to hotten up the coffee and bring these boys something to eat. Come on up and sit, boys. They'll be no shootin' this evenin' unless you start it."

"We won't," Matt said. "And coffee would be fine. You'll probably throw us off the place in about two minutes."

Bull chuckled. "I doubt it. Go on and eat, boys, while I go in and get me a bottle. Then we'll talk."

Bull came back out with a large tray containing plates piled high with food, fresh baked bread, a coffee pot with cups, and a bottle of whiskey for himself. "Eat," he told the brothers. "We can talk while you fill your bellies. What's on your minds, boys? You took an awful chance coming here this evening."

"We were on a trail above the road about an hour or so ago," Matt said, while Sam busied himself with eating. Sam's philosophy in a situation like this was if he was going to die, he might as well go out with a full belly. "Ben Connors, Big Dan Parker, Dick Laurin, and a couple more men, named Junior and Henry, came along. They reined up for a loose shoe, and their conversation was interesting, to say the least. According to them, both you and John Carlin want me dead. I'm just curious as to why."

Bull paused in his pouring of whiskey. The brothers could see the frown on his face in the dim lamplight. "I gave no orders to have you killed. None at all. And while I'm not a church-goin' man, I do

107

believe in the hereafter, and I'll stand in church, with the parson as witness, with my hand on a Bible and swear to that, boys.''

"That's good enough for me, Bull." Matt picked up a fork and fell to eating his supper.

"Mr. Sutton," Sam said, "why do you and Carlin hate each other so?"

Bull smiled. "You boys got an hour or so to listen?"

"We have all the time it takes," Sam said.

Bull set his whiskey aside and poured a mug of coffee. He settled his considerable bulk in the hide chair and said, "Me and John came out here within days of each other. From Missouri by way of Kentucky. We both had a lot in common, and for awhile I thought we could be friends. We're both orphans, both taken in by good Christian people and come to find out we'd been raised up within a hoot and a holler of one another. Problem is, I bought most of my cattle on the way out, and I said most, while John stole nearly all of his. And by him doin' so, I eventually got tarred with the same brush. And while I've been the mean ol' Bull o' the Woods around these parts, I ain't no rustler. Other cow critters tend to join up with a trailin' herd no matter what a drover does to prevent it.

"I'll admit that I didn't try very hard to make friends with John. Not after the first year or so. He just wasn't gonna have no part of it, and I was just too damn busy raisin' this brood of mine and seein' to the ranch and fightin' Injuns and outlaws and the like. And I didn't do too good of a job raisin' my kids.

108

I'll admit it even though it hurts. I figure I got one good one out of the bunch, and that's Connie. And give the devil his due, John has a good boy in Daniel. But them two is not gonna get hitched up. And that's my final word on the planned weddin'. But you didn't come out here to talk about my problems with Connie."

The brothers stopped eating for a moment and looked at each other. This sure didn't sound like the fire-eating Bull o' of the Woods they had met in town.

Bull caught their glances and smiled. "If that stupid fight between me and John did anything, it slapped some sense into my head. It gave me time to sit around the house and think, while I was groaning and moaning from all those licks John laid on me. I can't speak for John Carlin, only for myself. I've been forced to admit that I've got a pack of ornery, no-count kids . . . except for Connie." He glanced toward the living room. His wife nor none of his children were within earshot. "And my wife ain't had much to do with me in a long time. We have not slept in the same bed for over fifteen years." He smiled. "That, in itself, is enough to make a man right testy."

Matt and Sam smiled with him, both of them finding that they rather liked this bear of a man.

Bull said, "I got me a suspicion that my kids have been whisperin' to this pack of gunslicks I've surrounded myself with. They got something under-handed workin' in their heads. They think I don't know it." He took a sheet of paper from his pocket. "This is a list of the gunhandlers I've hired and how

109

much I owe them. I'm paying them off come the mornin', and puttin' word out that I am lookin' for cowboys. Unless I miss the mark, John will hire all that I fire."

"So the war is over?" Sam asked softly.

"As far as I'm concerned. But it won't be for John. You'll see. I'm gonna hire me some punchers that ride for the brand and herd cows. They'll know how to use a gun, but they won't be gunslingers. And when I do that, my kids are gonna turn against me . . . all except Connie. Stick around and see."

"Maybe if we rode over and talked to John?" Matt suggested.

Bull shrugged his massive shoulders. "Go ahead. But it won't do you any good. He might have you shot on sight. Now go ahead and ask the question that's burnin' your tongue to get out."

"Why the change of heart, Mr. Sutton?" Sam asked.

Bull stood up, and when Bull stood up, it seemed to take a full minute. He walked to the railing and looked out into the darkness. "I'm pushin' fifty hard, boys. I got everything, and I ain't got nothin'. A bunch of goddamn, no good, sneakin', connivin', back-stabbin' kids. A wife that just barely tolerates me. And that's my fault. I got maybe two or three real cowboys left on the range. I knew this . . . mess had to stop when Frank rode out the other day. Damn good cowboy. Been with me ten years. Almost as long as Laredo." He turned around. "You boys see any punchers lookin' for work, you send them to me. I've got to start workin' my range. And I'll find out who

110

told this pack of coyotes to kill you, Bodine. That's a promise. But I suspect it was my two oldest boys, Hugh and Randy. And young Ross was right in there with them, and my girls, too. Damn!"

"I don't mean this to sound sarcastic, Bull," Matt said. "But are you going to church come Sunday morning?"

Bull looked startled for a moment, and then busted out laughing. The laughter boomed and echoed around the yard. "An ol' sinner like me? No . . . I don't think I'm quite ready for that. The damn church roof might fall in on me. All that I've told you this night . . . you break it to Tom Riley gently. I don't want to be responsible for givin' the man a heart attack."

It was late when the brothers rode back into town, and Tom Riley's small house was dark and so was the marshal's office. The blood-bonded brothers stabled their horses, rubbed them down, and forked hay into the stalls for them. Just as they approached the yawning entrance to the big livery, Sam put out a hand and stopped his brother.

"What is it?" Matt whispered.

"A glint of light off metal. Across the street between Wo Fong's and the Mexican Cafe."

Matt instantly went to his right and Sam cut left, stepping away from the entrance and moving into the shadows behind the front wall. They waited silently. Not one light shone anywhere along either side of the main street of the town. Even the saloons

111

were closed and dark.

The glint might have come from a tin can or a discarded broken bit or spur. But the brothers weren't taking any chances. They waited.

They caught just the faintest murmur of a whisper, and then heard a boot scrape on the ground. Sam motioned to himself, and then to the rear of the cavernous building, and Matt nodded his understanding.

Sam vanished into the gloom. A figure dressed in dark clothing darted across the street, heading for a vacant building next to the livery. Matt heard boots strike with a hollow sound on the boardwalk, and he stepped outside and flattened against the front.

"You looking for me?" he called softly, and then hit the ground.

Twin guns boomed and sparked the night, and Matt fired directly between the muzzle blasts, then rolled to his right behind a pile of broken wheels, axles, and other busted wagon and buggy parts. Slugs slammed against the livery wall, and Matt and Sam fired as one.

"Damn!" came the anguished call from across the street. That was followed by the thud of a man hitting the ground.

Lamps were being turned on from one end of the town to the other, and Tom and a deputy were running up the street, both in various stages of undress.

"Head for cover, Tom!" Sam called. "We don't know how many there are."

Tom jumped behind a water trough, and Van

112

Dixon stopped and knelt down beside the high boardwalk.

A horse galloping away told the rest of the story. The one left had had enough for this night.

Both gunmen were still alive, and both had been stretched out beside each other on the boardwalk that ended at the livery and picked up again at Wo Fong's. But Doc Blaine shook his head at the unspoken questions in Tom's eyes.

"Who hired you to gun me?" Matt asked.

"Go to hell," the gutshot man gasped.

"I got their horses, Tom," Van said, leading two horses up to the livery door. "But I never seen these brands before. It's a double saddle riggin'. Probably Texas."

"Damn right," the other assassin said.

"You should have stayed there," Doc Blaine bluntly told the man. "Because both of you are going to be buried in Idaho Territory."

"That's disgustin'," the man said.

"What the hell difference do it make?" his dying partner asked. "We ain't gonna know it."

"Maybe you'll tell me who hired you?" Matt asked.

"When pigs fly like eagles, Bodine."

"Sutton or Carlin?" Sam asked.

"Nope. I can tell you that much for shore. And I ain't lyin' 'bout that. Gimmie some laudanum, Doc."

"You'll be dead before it could take effect, Mister," Doc Blaine told him.

"Name's Poe," the man whispered. "Hank Poe. I got money in my britches for a marker. Somebody see to that, will you?"

"We'll see to it."

Hank Poe closed his eyes and never opened them again.

"What's your name?" Tom asked the other gunny.

"John Smith. And don't laugh. It's the truth."

"You got anyone you want us to notify?"

"Naw. Just wrap me up good and bury me deep." He cut his fading eyes to Matt. "Poe was speakin' the truth to you, Bodine. It wasn't neither Sutton nor Carlin who hired us."

"Tell me who it was."

The gunman laughed out of his bloody mouth and shook his head. "You'll find out in time. But I know it all. I know the whole story. And it's a strange one. Mighty queer. You see, Bodine. There was . . . There was more than . . ." The man coughed up blood and began gasping for air. Blaine quickly cleared his throat. But it was to no avail. Smith's head lolled to one side.

"There was what?" Sam asked.

But Smith was dead.

"This thing is gettin' more twists and turns than a damn snake hole," Tom said.

"He knew the whole story," Sam mused. "How did he know it? Ben Connors admitted on the trail that he didn't."

"What about Ben Connors?" Tom asked.

"In the morning, Tom," Matt said. "You'd stay awake all night if we told you the news now."

"Now I'll stay awake all night just wondering what the news is," the marshal groused.

9

Over breakfast at the hotel, Marshal Tom Riley stared in disbelief at the words the brothers told him. He couldn't believe what he was hearing. Halfway through his eggs, young Parley ran in and whispered in Tom's ear.

"I gotta see it to believe it," Tom said. "Come on, boys."

On the porch of the hotel, the men watched as all the gunfighters from the Flying BS rode into town and reined up in front of the Carlin House.

"Looks like Bull meant every word he said," Tom muttered. "And he was right about John hirin' those bad ones as soon as Bull fired them. I applaud Bull for tryin' to end this years-long war, but he may have committed suicide by doin' it."

"Let's take a walk over to the Carlin House," Sam suggested. "The conversation should be quite lively."

"That's one way of puttin' it," Tom said.

As expected, the crowd in the saloon fell silent as soon as the marshal, the young deputy, and the brothers walked in. But the line of gunmen at the bar and seated at tables were a sullen-faced lot.

Bartender George looked awfully nervous.

Tom Riley walked straight up to Ben Connors, while Sam and Matt separated to better watch the room filled with some of the most notorious gunmen in the West. Parley stood to the right of the batwings. The deputy was young, but he had more than his share of sand.

"Make my day a delightful one and tell me you boys are pullin' out," Tom said to Ben.

The gunslick smiled. "Sorry to disappoint you, Marshal. But as of ten o'clock last night, more or less, we all went to work for the Circle JC spread. Bull suddenly got religion, or some such crap as that."

"What did his kids think about that?"

"Why don't you ask them, Marshal? I've never been one to carry tales. You care for a taste of Who Hit John?" He lifted his shot glass.

"It's a little early for me, Ben."

Ben sipped his drink and said, "A man should never refuse a free drink, Marshal. Never know when it might be his last one."

"I could take that as a threat, Ben."

"But you won't, 'cause it ain't."

Tom knew there was no point in pressing this gunfighter for details of what might be around the bend, or any of the other gunhandlers in the room, for that matter. All he could do was wait.

But he could put a crimp in their conversation and

116

gently push just a bit. Tom called for a pot of coffee and cups and took a table. Matt and Sam and the young deputy joined him.

They all noticed that George was very nervous as he set the tray on the table. His eyes looked haunted.

"That man is scared out of his wits," Sam whispered, after George had returned to his post behind the long bar. "He's overheard something."

"Yeah," Tom agreed softly. "But you'll never get anything out of him. He's John Carlin's man all the way. Look at them," Tom said, shifting his eyes. "Must be twenty-five or thirty of the randiest ol' boys west of the Mississippi in this room. Each man has ten to fifty dead men behind him. And here we sit, like bumps on a log, not able to do nothin'."

The batwings pushed open and three men, all of them looking to be in their thirties, stepped in. They were slightly bow-legged and their clothing trail-worn. They did not wear their guns like gunfighters, but carried them more like tools.

"Punchers," Matt said. "On the drift looking for work."

The cowboys walked to the bar and ordered beer. One of them said, "We're lookin' for work. Anybody around these parts hirin'?"

"A smart man would drift," Gene Baker said, a surly tone to his voice.

"Well," the lanky cowboy said. "I ain't never been known for my smarts. I'm just lookin' for work, not trouble."

"Trying the Flying BS," Tom called from the table.

117

"The what?" the cowboy asked, turning to look at the marshal.

Tom smiled. "Take the southwest fork at the hotel. It's not too far out of town. Man's name is Bull Sutton. He's hirin', so I hear."

"Much obliged, Marshal."

One of the young gunslicks looked at the trio of working cowboys and laughed nastily. "Would you boys just take a good look at them three saddlebums. This is gonna be as easy as target practice."

One of the cowboys, a short stocky man with flame red hair and freckles, and whose nickname just had to be Rusty, looked at the gunslick. "I ain't no hand with a short gun, sonny boy. But anytime you want to try me with fists, you just come on and throw your best punch."

"You boys finish your beers and walk on across the street to the Bull's Den if you want another one," Tom verbally stepped between impending trouble. "Or ride on out to Bull's spread." He looked at the loudmouth gunhandler. "As for you, you shut your goddamn mouth."

"Damn saddlebum challenged me," the surly gunslick said.

"He challenged you to fists," Tom said. "You want it, step up and toe the line. You pull iron on that puncher, and I'll shoot you myself."

The young punk muttered something under his breath and looked down at his shotglass. But he shut up.

The trio of cowboys knew they had ridden into trouble, but they'd seen that before. Besides, they were weary of riding the grub line and wanted a bunk house and a payday for work.

"The beer's on me," Bodine called to them.

"Thanks, friend," the redhead said. "My name's Rusty." He grinned easily. "But you probably figured that out already."

"Matt Bodine."

The cowboys looked at each other. They knew without being told that the man sitting with Bodine was Sam Two Wolves, the half-Cheyenne who was almost as good with a gun as his blood-brother. They also knew that when the blood-brothers were in an area, trouble seemed to pop up sudden like.

"Pleased," Rusty said. "This here's Hicks and the skinny one is Slim. Back when I was just a youngster, I rode right up on a band of Cheyenne. Like to have scared the bejesus out of me. I had a horse goin' lame and about ten cartridges in my belt. This real regal-lookin' man rode up even with me and said, 'Your horse is tired and you look hungry. Come with us.' Well, I shore figured I didn't have no choice in the matter. Come to find out, that was Medicine Horse. He and them others was out huntin' game, not trouble. They fed me right good, and we swapped horses. His son was with that bunch, and a white boy, too. Both of them about eight or nine years old. That would be Bodine and you, Mister Two Wolves."

"I remember," Sam said with a smile. "The women were fascinated by your red hair. You had nothing to fear. My father and those who followed him never harmed a white man who was friendly with them."

119

"Ain't that sweet?" another young gunslick had to pop off. "Makes me want to puke. I figure the only good Injun's a dead one."

Sam pushed back his chair and stood up, all in one fluid movement. He faced the mouthy punk. "You want to try to make this Indian a dead one?"

Tom opened his mouth.

"Stay out of it," Matt said quietly. "This is none of your affair."

Tom didn't like that one bit. But he nodded his head and remained silent. It's overdue, he thought. Way past time.

"Get up!" Sam spoke sharply. "Get up and let iron back up your big mouth."

It was all up to the mouthy gunslick now. He had but two choices: stand up and drag iron, or turn tail and run. He had been brought up to hate Indians. Brought up to feel that he was far superior to the red man. He looked up from his drink and saw behind all his prejudice and hate, saw the bottom line. Fear. And it infuriated him. He wasn't afraid of no damn Injun.

He slowly stood up. "No damn breed talks to me like that," he said, his words coming out hoarsely.

"Then shut my mouth," Sam said calmly. "You know how. Let's see if you can."

The other gunhands waited, all of them being careful to keep their hands in sight. Not out of fear, simply following the unwritten code of the time. A man saddles his own horses and stomps on his own snakes.

"Like stealin' a cookie from a baby," the young gunslick said.

"Yes," Sam said. "I'm sure you would know all about that."

The self-proclaimed gunfighter cursed Sam and grabbed for his guns, his face shiny with sweat and his eyes wild. Sam's hand flashed and his .44 roared, belching fire and smoke. The gunman never got his .45 clear of leather, the .44 slug striking him in the chest and knocking him backward. He coughed, cursed, and straightened up.

"Fast," Paul Stewart muttered. "Real fast."

Other hired guns in the room were thinking: Faster than me. A couple made up their minds right then that when the smoke cleared, they were gone from this area.

The young gunslinger lifted his .45 from leather and jacked the hammer back. With blood leaking from his mouth, and a curse on his lips, he leveled the Colt.

Sam shot him again, the big .44 slug taking him in the belly and doubling him over. The kid rocked back on his bootheels and sat down hard on the floor. The .45 dropped from his hand and went off when it landed on the hardwood, the slug gouging a hole in the boards.

"I don't believe it!" the mortally wounded young man gasped. "A damn Injun beat me to the draw." He fell over and started yelling as the white-hot pain struck him hard.

No one made a move to help the dying man. No

one did anything with their hands except keep them still.

Doc Blaine had heard the shots and came on a run, as did the mortician and his helper. Blaine pushed open the batwings and walked through the gunsmoke to the fallen man. He knelt down and tried to unbutton the man's bloody shirt. The kid pushed his hands away.

"Just as well," Blaine muttered.

"About five-nine," the mortician said. "I think we have one that will do nicely."

"You go to hell," the dying man said.

Matt and Tom had stood up. Sam punched out empties and reloaded full.

"You have any money?" the mortician asked, squatting down beside the dying would-be gunslick.

"I want a gospel shouter to pray over me," the kid gasped.

Sam turned his back to the dying man and started walking toward the batwings.

"By God!" Gene Baker shouted, shoving back his chair and standing up. "I'll not let this go unavenged. Turn around and face me, you goddamn greasy Injun!" He was dragging iron as he spoke.

Sam drew as he turned, and the entire room exploded in gunfire as other gunnies pulled pistols and Matt and Tom and young Parley did the same. Doc Blaine, the undertaker, and his helper flattened out on the floor, and all three said a prayer that no one would shoot low. George hit the boards behind the bar, crouching behind a barrel of beer. This was probably the most dangerous situation he'd been in

122

since he'd left his wife and kids back in St. Louis and headed for the Wild West. George had questioned the wisdom of that many times, but never so much as in these lead-flying seconds.

Gene Baker took a .44 just below the throat and was flung backward by the shock of it. He leaned against a post and tried to return the fire, but the blood was gushing from the horrible wound, and his gun was slick with it. He could not cock his pistol; his thumb kept slipping off the hammer.

"Damn your eyes," Gene gasped as he used his left hand to cock the .45.

Norm Meeker lifted his .45 and fired just as Gene lurched to one side. The slug caught him in the back of the head and blew out one eye.

"Oh, my God!" Norm yelled.

Gene dropped like a rock and landed on top of the dying kid, bringing a wild shriek of pain.

Matt lined up Norm and put a .44 slug right between the man's eyes just as Tom fired and dropped a gunslick dead to the floor. The kid whose mouth had brought all this on wrapped his hand around the butt of a .45 that had fallen from Gene's hand and let loose one round. The slug tore through the bar and punched a hole in the barrel of beer. George let out a yelp and crawled on hands and knees to another location behind the bar.

Rambling Ed Clark quickly sized up the situation and dived headfirst through a window and rolled off the boardwalk, wanting no part of this close-in gunfight.

Matt, Sam, Tom, and Parley had dropped to the

floor, behind the dubious protection of tables, which had about as much chance of stopping a .44 or .45 slug as an elephant doing the ballet.

A half dozen gunhands crawled on hands and knees into the storeroom and out the back door. Others were stretched out on the floor taking no part in the shootout in the Carlin House. Their thinking was that they didn't owe that damn stupid loud-mouth kid anything. And anyone who would open a dance in a close barroom was totally ignorant.

Deputies Van Dixon and Nate Perry ran up to the shattered windows of the saloon with Greeners in their hands, saw where their friends were, and cut loose at anyone standing up. The effects were terrible at the close range. Big Ed MacGreagor took a full load in the chest and was sent spinning across the room. He slammed against the upright piano, and his wildly jerking fingers played a horrible tune as the life left his buckshot shattered body.

Bob Lortin took a full blast from a sawed-off ten-gauge in the face, and his head disappeared. Paul Stewart, Simon Green, and Ned Kerry jumped behind the bar, and Paul landed right on top of George, knocking the wind out of the bartender.

A wild bullet sailed across the street and knocked a hole in the coffee grinder of the general store. Another slug whined down the street and ruined a bolt of cloth in Miss Charlotte's Fashionable Gowns.

Men and women and kids and dogs and cats and chickens were yelling and screaming and barking and shrieking and clucking and running in all directions up and down the street.

Rev. William Fowler and his wife, Melinda, who had been out calling on the Godless and other residents of the town who they felt needed a good dose of the Lord, jumped into the Bull's Den as the lead started flying and stretched out on the floor. They stared up in horror at a painting of a nude lady hanging behind the bar.

Back in the Carlin House, Tom Riley yelled above the roar of gunfire, "I command you all to cease and desist in the name of the law!"

His words got his hat blown off his head. He leveled his pistol and drilled the gunman about two inches above the belt buckle.

A shopkeeper leaned out of his store, sighted in with his shotgun, and blasted away at the running Ramblin' Ed Clark as the man tried to reach the livery and his horse. A few of the birdshot caught the gunman in the butt, and he hollered and jumped into an alley.

Paul Brown, Big Dan Parker, and J.B. Adams crawled out of the saloon, on their bellies, and slipped out the back door. They wanted no part of this craziness.

Utah Bates, Henry Rogers, and Bob Coody were others who took no part in the shooting. They had all run into a storeroom and slammed the door.

As quickly as the shooting began, it ended. Those outlaws who had taken part in the gunplay were either dead or dying. Slowly, those on the side of the law stood up, their hands filled with .44s and .45s.

"You boys who took no part in this hit the air," Tom said, then coughed from the thick gunsmoke that smarted the eyes and burned the throat.

"We're gone, Tom," Jack Norman said, standing up from his belly-down position on the floor. The remaining gunhands rose from behind tables and off the floor and trooped out. They wasted no time in exiting the town.

Doc Blaine and the undertaker and his helper rose up to their knees and looked around at all the carnage the few moments of gunplay had produced. Doc Blaine glanced over at young Parley, who was punching out empties and loading up his guns. "Get some men in here to help carry the badly wounded out," he said. "Where's my bag?" he asked, looking around him.

"Help me, Doc," a wounded gunhand moaned.

"George," Tom called. "George! Damnit, get out here with some sawdust and cover up this blood. It's slippery as an icehouse in here."

A man wearing an expensive suit and low-heeled shoes stepped into the barroom. Neither Matt nor Sam had ever seen this citizen before. He shook his head at the sight.

"Mr. Singer," Tom said. "Good to have you back. How was your trip?"

"Fine, Tom. Just fine," the big man replied, his eyes touching the blood brothers. A smile was on his lips, but his eyes were cold and hostile. "New deputies, Tom?"

"Young Parley is. And Nate and Van. These are friends of mine. Matt Bodine and Sam Two Wolves. This is Miles Singer, boys. Owns the bank and a right nice spread north of town."

126

The brothers nodded their greetings, then looked at each other, their secret suspicions now almost solidly confirmed. The town of Crossville a.k.a. Carlin-Sutton held quite a mystery, and the brothers held the key to the long locked door.

Now all they had to do was stay alive long enough to open it.

10

"A lot of speculation with no proof, brother," Sam said.

"Has to be, though," Matt replied.

The brothers had saddled up and ridden out of town, to sit and talk by the side of a little creek about a mile from the town. There was no way anyone could slip up on them to eavesdrop.

"So of the three men, how many of them know the truth?"

Matt chewed on a blade of grass for a moment. "Singer, for sure. Maybe John Carlin. I think Bull is totally in the dark."

"Their kids?"

"Ah, now that might be a possibility."

Sam chunked a stone into the creek. "And what business it is of ours?"

"Absolutely none."

They were silent for a moment, Sam finally saying, "So who do we tell of our suspicions?"

"No one," Matt said. "At least, not yet."

"Agreed. We sure have no proof, and a gut-hunch won't stand up in court."

The brothers looked at one another and grinned, mischief shining in their eyes.

"We could have some fun," Sam suggested.

"You have an evil mind, Redskin," Matt said.

"Evil is contagious. So I probably caught it from you."

The brothers rode back to town, both of them reining down in front of the telegraph office. They sent their wires and then went back to their room at the hotel and sat by the window overlooking the main street. They waited for the fireworks to start.

They watched as the telegrapher locked up his office and hustled over to the bank.

"Just like we thought he would," Sam said. "You know, there is yet another person who just might be involved in this mystery."

"Ladue," Matt said.

"Very good, brother. Yes. But how and why?"

"How, I don't know. Why, might be that if he sits back, he might pick up some of the pieces after the big blow. I got the feeling that he wasn't leveling with us that day we talked at length."

"He's crazy, you know?"

"I picked up on that. He just might feel—like a few of those old mountain men do—that since he was here first, all this belongs to him. Mountain fever might have got him."

"All right, answer me this: who are the gunfighters really working for?"

Matt slowly built a cigarette, licked it and lit. "I'd say that some of them are really on John's payroll. The majority of them are working for Singer."

"Agreed. Must have thrown a kink into things when Bull fired his pack."

"And didn't Tom say that Singer came back early from his trip?"

"Yes. He was supposed to have been gone several weeks. If I had to take a guess, I'd say that J.B. Adams is Singer's front man in all this. He got word to Singer through the telegraph office. Unless Ben Connors was lying that evening back on the trail."

"And what about Tom Riley?"

"Do you trust him?"

"Yes, and no. Tom's not a young man any longer. He might be thinking about his future and sees a pretty bleak road ahead of him. But that's just speculation."

"We're thinking alike. Brother, we are in a very dangerous spot in all this."

Matt nodded his head. "Here's something else, too: I don't think we could ride out even if we wanted to."

"Nor do I. I started getting a funny feeling yesterday afternoon that we were being watched."

"Remember that play we saw last year? The mystery?"

"Yes. What? . . . Oh, yes. The plot, it doth thicken."

"Let's don't let it get too thick," Matt said. "It's tough getting out of quicksand."

* * *

The brothers were conscious of being followed, and whoever was paying the men had obviously told them to be certain the brothers were aware of it. Matt and Sam decided to make the best of it and try to ignore their followers. But it was done with an effort.

Bank drafts that the brothers had wired for came in on the stage from Wells Fargo, and Miles Singer's eyes bugged out when the young men deposited the checks at his bank.

"You boys, ah, planning on investing in property around here?" the banker questioned.

"Hadn't thought about that," Sam said.

"We just like to have ample spending money," Matt added with a smile. "We can be real big spenders. You're sure the money will be safe in your bank?"

"Oh, my, yes!" Singer said. "That's the finest safe in all of Idaho Territory."

"That makes me feel better already," Sam said, and the brothers left the bank, both of them carrying a large amount of cash, in paper and gold coin.

"Now you can tell me your plan for doing this?" Sam said, once on the boardwalk.

"What plan?"

Sam pulled up short. "The plan, the reasoning for this transfer of funds and for us walking around with too damn much money on us."

"Oh, I don't have a plan. I just thought it might stir things up some."

"You don't have a . . ." Sam bit back his words and sighed. "Why doesn't that surprise me?"

Matt just grinned at him and walked on. They

watched as Laredo and Rusty rode into town and up to the Bull's Den. Several tired horses, showing the signs of a long ride, were tied at the rail. The brothers walked over and inside.

Laredo waved at them and motioned them up to the bar. He grinned and stuck out his hand, and the brothers shook it. "Man, I can't begin to tell you boys how nice it is now out to the ranch. The boss ain't got a gunslick on the payroll, and these here ol' boys is just signin' on. Boys," he turned to the punchers at the bar. "This here is Matt Bodine and Sam Two Wolves. Sutton, Hal, Patton, and Gamble."

"So the Bull really meant it when he said the war was over?" Sam asked.

"You bet your boots he did. And them no-count kids of his was mad about that. All but Connie. She's a fine girl. But Ross and Hugh and Randy . . . whew, boys, they was some hot."

"But not mad enough to leave home?" Matt said with a smile.

"Oh, no. They know what side their biscuits is buttered on. But I don't trust none of them. I shouldn't be talkin' family stuff to you boys, but the Bull sorta admires your nerve and likes the both of you. He said if I seen you to tell you to come out whenever you've a mind to. The coffee's always hot."

"Tell him we appreciate that, and we'll do it. But it might not be a wise thing to do with us being followed all the time," Matt said.

"Them two hardcases across the street?" Hal spoke up.

"That's two of them, yes," Sam said. "They work

in teams."

"That's Dud Mackin and Butch Proctor," the cowboy said. "I knew 'em down Moab way. They're bad ones. Back-shooters and sneak thieves. They usually ride with a heavy set fellow called Donner. Looks like he needs a shave all the time."

"He's one of them, all right," Matt said, signaling for a beer. Sam shook his head at the offer. Matt described the other three of the six men they had spotted.

"They don't ring no bell with me," Hal said. "But you can bet if they're workin' with Proctor and Mackin and Donner, they're bad ones."

"Where are they stayin'?" Laredo asked.

"At the hotel," Sam told him. "All six of them."

"That's odd," Laredo said. "I ain't never knowed John to put up nobody at the hotel. Not even cattle buyers. They all stay out at his house. Maybe they ain't workin' for the Circle JC."

"Then . . . ?" Matt trailed that off.

Laredo shrugged his shoulders. "You got me. This thing just keeps gettin' queerer and queerer."

Laredo and the new men finished their beers and rode out for home range. Matt and Sam walked out on the boardwalk in time to seen John Carlin and his brood come riding into town, the girls in a buggy, flanked on both sides by hired guns, all of them kicking up unnecessary dust.

"The parade comes to town," Sam muttered. He looked at Johnny Carlin as the young man swung down from the saddle. "Complete with court jester.

Brother, if those yahoos following us aren't working for his lord and majesty there, who are they working for?"

"Singer, I guess. I think Ladue would handle his own affairs if it came to that. And I'm still not sure which side he's on. If he's on any side."

"He is," Sam said confidently. "His own side."

John Carlin glanced over at the brothers and gave them a cold look before turning his back to them and walking into the Carlin House, followed by half a dozen gunmen. His daughter and wife walked to the general store and stepped inside, the rest of the hired guns with them. The brothers walked across the street.

"Well now," Sam said, looking down the street toward the fork in the road. "Things are about to get real interesting."

Hugh, Randy, and Ross Sutton were riding slowly into town. Johnny, Clement, and Pete Carlin stood on the boardwalk in front of the Carlin House and watched them. The Carlin brothers all slipped the hammer-thongs from their holstered pistols, a move that did not escape the eyes of Matt and Sam.

Two of the Sutton boys reined up in front of the Bull's Den and swung down. They gave the blood brothers a mean glance and stepped inside the saloon. Hugh had reined in by the saddle shop and strangely had disappeared into the alley. Matt watched the action, curious.

Young Parley walked up, a worried look on his face. "Tom and Van rode out early this morning," he

135

said. "Rustlers hit one of the smaller spreads south of here. Nate's gone out to a farmer's place to talk to him about a horse being stolen. Can I count on you boys to help me if trouble starts?"

"You know you can," Sam assured the young deputy.

Matt was paying little attention, his gaze on the mouth of the alley. His eyes narrowed as the heavy-set Donner stepped out and looked up and down the street before heading into the Carlin House.

"What the hell?" Matt muttered, as Hugh stepped out of the alley, stood for a moment, and then walked up the boardwalk, turning in at the bank. "This stew is getting a little thick," Matt murmured to himself. Sam and Parley had walked off a few feet and did not hear Matt's comments.

Hugh exited the bank and strolled up to the Bull's Den, looking over at Matt before pushing open the batwings. Before Matt could say anything to Sam or Parley, the Carlin brothers stepped out of the saloon across the street, guns drawn.

"Come on out and let's settle this now!" Johnny yelled. "Come on out, you Sutton bastards!"

"Move, feet!" Sam said, and the brothers and the deputy vacated that area as quickly as possible.

The boardwalk in front of the Carlin House was crowded with Carlins and hired guns, John Carlin standing near the boardwalk's end near the alley, where Matt and Sam and Parley were waiting and watching.

"Draw, you bastards!" Johnny yelled, and the

quiet air was filled with gunfire.

Windows were smashed, chunks of board were gouged out, and horses were rearing up and screaming, tearing loose from the hitchrails in fright.

But nobody seemed to be hitting anything except air and glass and wood. Then Matt saw Marcel turn, an evil grin on his lips, and point his pistol at his father. Matt lunged, grabbed the man by the boots and jerked him off the boardwalk just as Marcel fired. The slug howled harmlessly off into the air, and John Carlin hit the ground hard, knocking the wind from him.

Marcel had turned and was once more firing at the Sutton brothers. And just like everybody else, was hitting nothing.

"What the hell?" John Carlin yelled, struggling to get up from the ground.

"Stay down, you damn fool," Matt told him. "Your own son just tried to kill you."

"I don't believe that!"

"Why would I lie?" Matt asked calmly, over the cracking of pistol fire. "Look at them, John. They're all standing out in the open and not a damn one of them is hitting anything. Does that tell you something?"

John Carlin sat up, his butt still on the ground, and looked at what was evident now as a mock battle. He turned his eyes to Matt. "What in the hell is going on here?"

"Break this up right now!" Parley yelled. "Or we start shooting. Get back in the damn saloons."

The firing stopped as if on cue, and the would-be warriors stepped back into the saloons.

"Now that was just too easy," Parley commented, holstering his pistol. He and Sam stepped up onto the boardwalk.

"Don't turn your back on Marcel," Matt whispered. "Or any of your other kids, for that matter. I think your kids and Bull's kids are all in this thing together. And there is a whole lot more, too. It's complicated."

John stared at him for a moment, then shook his head and heaved himself to his boots and, now standing, took a long and disbelieving look at the deserted street. "My boys are all crack shots. And so aer Bull's boys. Those gunfighters are expert marksmen. Yet nobody hit anything." He turned eyes that were now not quite so hostile toward Matt. "You claim you saved my life. Maybe you did. I reckon we've got to talk."

"You and me and Sam and Bull. My brother and I have a theory. One hour before sunset, by that creek just south of town where the beaver have the dam. Agreed?"

The man hesitated for a moment, and then said, "Agreed." John brushed the dirt off his jeans and shirt.

"Is that young man with your wife your son Daniel?"

"Yes."

"Stay with him. And bring him with you to the creek. I think he's the only one of your kids you can trust."

"I hope to God you're talkin' nonsense, Bodine."

"I'm not. But you'd better brace yourself. What Sam and me have to say is going to come as a real shock to both you and Bull."

"Not no more than that put-up fight I just witnessed."

"I wouldn't count on it," Matt said drily.

11

When Matt got Sam off to himself, he told him what had transpired and asked him to ride for Bull's spread and have him meet them at the creek, and to say nothing to anyone else. Especially any of his kids.

"Incredible," Sam said.

John Carlin told his family and hired guns to head back to the ranch and cool off, having said the latter rather drily and with more than a note of sarcasm. Daniel stayed with his father in town, both of them on the pretense of having business to take care of.

All the parties concerned met at the creek about an hour before sundown. John and Bull stood glaring at each other, a few yards apart, absolutely no love lost between them. But at Matt's request, they had looped their gunbelts over their saddlehorns.

"This had better be good, boys," Bull said. "I got supper waiting, and it's a fine one."

"Damn waste of time if you ask me," John grumbled.

"No doubt about it in my mind," Sam said, after looking first at John and then at Bull.

"Nor mine," Matt said. "Let's sit, gentlemen. Nature placed these logs just perfect for that."

Matt spoke four words, and the two ranchers came off the logs as if propelled out of a cannon.

"We're what?" Bull screamed.

"You're out of your goddamn mind!" John shouted.

"Oh, there's more," Sam picked it up. "There were three of you. Singer is another."

Both men sat down on the logs so hard their teeth clicked together. Daniel Carlin and Connie Sutton moved closer together and held hands. Their faces were pale.

"Go squat down by the creek and look at your reflections in the water together," Matt urged them. "Go on. Do it."

Reluctantly, the ranchers moved to the creek and knelt down, staring at their reflections. They looked at each other, then back at their reflections.

"Both orphans, right?" Sam asked.

"Yeah," Bull said, his tone softer. "We came from the same part of the country. But I knew my mother. Her name was Estelle."

"And my mother's name was Claire," John said.

"How about your fathers?" Matt asked.

"I don't know anything about him," Bull said. "Except he was a big bear of a man with dark curly hair."

"Same with me," John said. "Mother said he was a big strong man. I had an older brother, I know that.

142

But I never saw him. I have no idea where he might be." He looked at Bull. "My mother said my father had dark curly hair. Were you a woods colt, Bull?"

"Yeah."

"Me, too."

Bull smiled ruefully. "Poppa got around, didn't he?"

"Looks like it. We do kinda resemble, Bull."

"I have to say that's right. And come to think of it, Singer bears a strong likeness to us. You trust your kids, John?" he asked abruptly.

"Hell, no! At least not after today. I been doin' some strong thinkin', too. And I think my kids are playin' me for a sucker."

"Yeah, me, too," Bull said with a sigh. "But I have to say that since I fired all those damn gunhands, my wife and I have, ah, well, ah . . . You know what I mean. We're, ah, closer."

John grinned at him. "My wife hasn't had much to do with me for some years, Bull. You reckon if I fired those gunslicks it might improve my situation at home?"

"It damn sure did for me."

John nodded his big head. He looked at his son. "Dan, this then is what you've been tryin' to tell me for some time. My kids are traitors toward me, right?"

"I'm afraid so, Dad. But I don't know if you can fire those gunfighters."

"You want to explain that, boy?"

The young man looked over at Matt. Matt said, "They might just laugh in your face, John. For I have a hunch they're working for your kids, Bull's kids, and for Singer."

"What a sorry damn mess!" Bull said.

"Dad," Connie said. "If you and Mr. Carlin are half brothers . . . what does that make Dan and me?"

"Half first cousins," Sam told her. "No . . . full second cousins." He was thoughtful for a moment. "No . . . I'm going to have to think about this for awhile."

"What it means is, havin' kids just might be chancy," Bull said. "But, hell, people marry first and second cousins all the time." He sighed. "I ain't got no objections to you two gettin' hitched. You, John?"

"Not a one. You have my blessin's." He laughed out loud and slapped his knee. "Bull, can you just imagine a hundred years from now someone tryin' to look up this family tree!"

Bull looked at him and busted out laughing.

Connie glanced at Dan. "Do I call your father 'Poppa' or 'Uncle John'?"

That set both fathers off again, and they laughed until tears were running down their eyes.

The laughter stopped abruptly when Bull's hat was blown off his head, and a rifle slug spat bark into John's face. Everybody hit the ground, pistols in hand.

"I told you we should have met at that other spot, brother," Sam said.

"Don't gloat," Matt said. "It doesn't become you."

"I'm not gloating, I assure you. I landed in a damn mud puddle."

John chuckled at the expression on Sam's face.

"You OK, son?"

"Fine, Dad."

"You all right, baby?" Bull called to his daughter.

"I'm fine, Dad. I just wish I could get to my rifle."

John grinned at his new-found half brother. "She'll do, Bull. She'll do."

Bull returned the grin and then jacked back the hammer on his .45, looking around for a target.

Matt tossed Connie a pistol, and she caught it and deftly spun the cylinder, checking for loads.

"Now I feel better," she said.

Dan tried to shift positions, and a bullet whistled past his head, so close he could feel the deadly heat. "Don't anybody try to move," he called softly. "They've got us down cold."

Matt saw what he thought was a boot sticking out from behind a thick stand of brush and aimed about two feet up from the boot. He squeezed off a round, and a wild shriek of pain ripped the late afternoon air.

"Oh, Christ! My knee's tore up bad! Oh, God, it hurts. Somebody get me out of here and to a sawbones."

John and Bull fired as one, and the shrieking stopped as the bullets found their mark. The ambusher did not need a doctor anymore.

Sam suddenly rolled to his right and reached the safety of rocks, leaving in his wake a hail of gunfire and bullets ripping up the ground inches behind him.

"Watch the breed," a familiar voice called. "He's gonna try slippin' up around us."

145

"Clement," John whispered, his voice shaky. "My own son is tryin' to kill me."

"Hell with the others," another all-too-familiar voice called out. "Kill John and Bull."

Bull turned anguished eyes toward John. "Randy," he whispered hoarsely. "Dear God in Heaven, what kind of kids did we produce?"

"Well, it's all out in the open now," John said. "We can legally kick them out."

"How?" Matt questioned. "All we've heard are voices. None of us have seen anybody. No judge would honor that."

John and Bull both did some fancy cussing.

"It'll be dark in about thirty minutes," Connie called. "If we can hold out 'til then, we have a chance."

"Somebody kill that bitch!" a wild voice screamed from outside the little earth-depression where the party was trapped.

"Ross," Bull said, the words tinged with bitterness. "My youngest son. Who wants to kill his sister." His sigh was clearly audible to the others.

Connie put a round in the general direction of her brother's voice.

"Holy cow!" Ross yelled. "I damn near got shot."

Connie carefully placed another round, and her brother bellered out his surprise and shock.

"Are you hit?" yet another voice was added.

"Marcel," John said.

"No," Ross called. "But if it'd been an inch closer, I'd a been dead."

John emptied his pistol at the brush where

Marcel's voice had sprung. Wild cussing cut the fading light, and the sound of boots hitting the ground came to those pinned down.

Sam's guns began roaring, and a man began screaming in pain. Matt chose that time to roll to his left and into a thin stand of cottonwoods. He came to his knees just as an unfamiliar face about twenty-five feet away turned toward him, eyes wide with surprise.

They were not surprised for long as Matt put a .44 slug between the gunhand's eyes. His head snapped back, and the hired gun stretched out on the ground.

"That's it!" a voice yelled. "Let's get out of here."

Seconds later, the sounds of fast-running horses were fading from the area.

"That was my son Pete who yelled that last bit," John said, walking to Matt's side in the trees. "The traitorous little shit!"

"I've never seen any of these people," Bull called, standing over the body of a dead gunny. "Somebody's brought in men and kept them hidden out."

"Who the hell can we trust?" John asked, as the group gathered by the man Sam had filled with lead.

"If these words had come out of my mouth this morning," Bull said. "Somebody would have had me put in the loony bin. But, John, I reckon we can trust each other."

John nodded his big head and stuck out his hand. Bull took the peace offering.

"I don't know how to handle this," John said. "What do I say to my kids when I get back home? How do I act?"

The sounds of horses galloping turned the group around. About ten minutes of light remained. Tom Riley reined up and jumped down from the saddle, Van Dixon with him. "We heard the shooting," Tom said. "What the hell's going on here?"

"We were ambushed," Matt said quickly, before anyone else could speak. "We were meeting out here to call an end to the war and someone slipped up on us. None of us ever got a glimpse of a face."

"You don't have any idea as to who it might have been?" Tom asked.

"Not a clue," Bull said.

"Nothing," John added.

Tom looked at both men. He took a longer, closer look, then he shook his head. "You know, I don't want to start a fight between you two, but I just now noticed something: you two damn sure resemble." He quickly held up a hand. "Now, don't fly off the handle at me. Lots of folks resemble. I was just voicin' a thought, that's all."

Sam took a chance and said, "They should resemble, Tom. They're half brothers."

Tom Riley's mouth dropped open, and he leaned up against a tree, clearly stunned by Sam's remark. "Brothers!" he blurted.

Van Dixon stood speechless, staring first at Bull, then at John.

Bull sized up the man as being genuinely shocked and said, "Matt and Sam put it together, Tom. Up until a few seconds ago, none of us really knew what side you stood on. Now I reckon you're neutral. It was our kids who ambushed us."

"Your . . . kids?" Tom said. He quickly recovered and looked at Matt and Sam. "All right, smart boys, you tell me what the hell is going on?"

Quickly and succinctly, Sam leveled with the man. The marshal was so shaken by the revelations he had to look around and find a large rock to sit on.

"Jesus, Mary, and Joseph," he muttered. He took off his hat and fanned himself. "I ain't ready for this. And you think Miles Singer is also your brother?"

"Yes," Bull spoke. "The resemblance is just too uncanny to be coincidence. But it took Matt and Sam here to point that out to us. He's got the same Kentucky drawl as me and John. Same features, same build, same everything, including being totally unreasonable about damn near anything and stubborn as a Missouri mule."

Tom nodded his head in absolute agreement with the last remark.

"We think the kids of Bull and John, with the exception of Dan and Connie here, are in this with Singer, and the gunfighters are working for them," Sam said.

Tom stuck his hat back on his head and stood up. "And you really didn't see any of the men who attacked you today?"

"No," John said. "But me and Bull know the voices of our sorry kids, and the boys were damn sure here taking part in it. I heard Clement and Marcel and Bull heard Randy and Ross."

"That's no good in a court of law."

"We know it," Bull said. "John, I got a plan. You better stay in town tonight, and I'll ride in in the morning, and we'll meet at Lawyer Sprague's office at say, oh, nine o'clock. I'm changing my will leaving everything to Connie and Roz and adding that under no circumstances will any of the other kids get any part of the ranch or my money, no matter what happens. I think Sprague can set it up so it's ironclad. You do the same, and then we'll have Tom and his deputies ride out to your place, and you can order the gunhands out. What do you say?"

"Sounds good to me. And just as soon as the gunhands leave, I'm kicking all my kids out except for Daniel."

"The girls, too?" Tom asked, worry on his face.

"They're in it just as strong as the boys," Dan said. "Connie and I have known it for months."

Both Bull and John did some cussing and kicking and stomping around for a moment. Bull said, "I'll give 'em all some money to tide them over. I'll set up accounts in Denver for them all. But from this moment on, I disown them all."

"Denver sounds good to me, too," John said. "What do we do about Singer?"

"I don't know. Let's face that after we deal with our no-count kids."

"You going to be all right this night, Bull?"

"Oh, yeah. I'll ride in the back way and brief the boys in the bunkhouse. I've got the makings of a good crew, and Laredo is rock-solid." He stuck out his hand, and John took it. "We've got years of catching up to do, brother. I look forward to goin' fishin' and huntin' with you."

John grinned. "Me, too, brother. Me, too!"

12

Lawyer Sprague was a sour-faced man, but one that kept his mouth shut about his clients and knew the law. He didn't blink an eye at the will changes. He drew them up, the men signed them, Matt and Sam witnessed the documents, and that was that.

Tom Riley left Nate Perry to look after things in town and took Parley and Van with him. Bull and Matt and Sam rode with John back to the Circle JC. It was a grim-faced group of men who rode up to the house of John Carlin. John had told his wife everything when he had returned home from the meeting and the ambush attempt, and she had been horrified at the behavior of her children, and then pleased to learn the war and the feud was, at long last, over.

"But what about the girls?" she had questioned.

"I won't leave them penniless. I'll set up trust funds so they won't starve or walk around with their drawers showing through ragged dresses, but they'll by God have to find work."

"But they're not trained to do anything!"

"That, Ginny, is their problem."

John had stopped by the bank to line his pockets with cash money to pay off the gunhands, and both he and Bull had closed out their accounts with Miles Singer, and withdrawn all their funds, leaving the man in damn near a state of cold-sweat shock and the bank very nearly void of ready cash. Miles was going to have to sink a lot of his own funds into the bank's coffers just to prevent a run once the news got out. And even that might not keep the man solvent.

Dan Carlin had taken his mother to the upstairs of the mansion and was guarding her against a possible attack by his brothers and sisters and the hired guns. Ginny Carlin called it an impossible situation. But she was scared, although she tried to keep that fear from the one son she knew was mentally stable.

The other sons and daughters of John and Ginny Carlin sat in the living room downstairs and waited for their father to make an appearance. They were sullen and scared, and no amount of tough talk or bravado could hide that. The girls were weepy and the boys grim-faced. The same scene was being played out at the BS spread, but without nearly as much tension, for over there, tough, straight-arrow cowboys, led by Laredo, were all over the house, keeping a wary eye on Bull's turncoat kids.

"You can't do this!" Wanda squalled at Slim.

"Doin' it," the lanky puncher replied.

"Get out of my house!" Willa yelled at Laredo.

"I take orders from Mrs. Sutton," the newly

promoted foreman told the young woman. "Not you."

Cleat and Shorty were outside, and Laredo expected trouble from them, for he had a suspicion they were secretly on the payroll of Singer.

"I don't think you can take me," Hugh Sutton told Rusty.

"Maybe not," the redheaded, freckle-faced cowboy said. "But I'll damn sure get lead in you on my way down."

Connie sat with her mother upstairs, a sawed-off, double-barreled shotgun across her jeans-clad knees. Extra shells were in her pocket.

"You simply must start wearing dresses," her mother told her. "Men's britches are not proper for a young lady."

"Hell with proper," Connie replied. "You have a fine figure, Mamma. You want to get Poppa's attention, slip into a pair of my jeans. That'll perk him up real quick."

"Heavens!" the mother said, but she had to hide a smile. Of late, all she had to do was walk into a room to get the Bull's attention. It was sort of like a second honeymoon. "I'm scared, daughter."

"It'll be all right, Momma. Everything will be all right."

"You're all fired," John told the gunhands gathered in the front yard. "Line up over yonder to draw your pay. The war is over, and I don't need you no more."

"I run this spread!" Johnny shouted from the front

153

porch. "Don't you men pay no attention to him. You all work for me."

"You don't run nothin', boy," the father told him coldly. "And you can pack up your junk and get gone with them."

"What?" the oldest son blurted.

"There ain't nothin' wrong with your ears. You heard me." John swung down from the saddle, and those with him did the same, spreading out across the yard.

"Oh, Daddy!" Petunia called from the porch. "I've been just worried sick about you. I'm so glad to see you home safely."

John cut cold eyes to his daughter. "Pack your crap, too, girl," he wiped the smirk from her face. "I will not abide something like you under my roof. Lars!" he called to one of the few cowboys left on the place. "Are you with me or against me?"

"Solid with you, boss," the hand called.

"Hitch up the buggy and drive Miss Petunia into town when she's ready."

"Right, boss."

"But . . . Daddy!" Petunia squalled.

"Hush up your mouth and pack," John told her.

J.B. Adams and Ben Connors sized up the situation quickly. Everything had gone sour out here, and there was no point in kicking up a fuss about it. Parley and Van held sawed-off shotguns in their hands, the hammers back. Matt Bodine was looking square at him, and Sam Two Wolves was facing Ben. Tom Riley was staring hard at Rambling Ed Clark, and Bull Sutton was holding a rifle aimed smack at

Yok Zapata's belly. He cut his eyes to the second floor of the ranch house. Daniel Carlin was aiming a rifle at Dick Yandle's chest, and Ginny Carlin was aiming a rifle at Phillip Bacque, and Bacque was well aware of it. The percentages were all wrong here, J.B. thought. Best thing to do was draw their pay and ride into town.

"I'll get my gear from the bunkhouse, John," J.B. said.

"Fine, J.B.," John said.

"By God, I won't," Utah Bates said.

"Don't be a fool, boy," Bacque told him. He put both hands in his back pockets and turned to face Ginny Carlin's rifle. "I am out of this, Mrs. Carlin. I am going to pack my possessions and then draw my time."

He turned and walked toward the bunkhouse, most of the others following him. Only the younger, less wise ones stayed put, facing the line of lawmen, ranchers, and the blood brothers.

"You see!" Clement called from the porch. "Them's workin' for us, Pa. It's you who'd better pack your war bag and get gone from here."

"Clement," John said, steel in his words. "You got a couple of choices. And I'll name them. Either pack and get out, or fill your hand."

The expression on the young man's face was clear shock. His own father was telling him to draw down. He couldn't believe it.

"Back off," Johnny said low. "He's holdin' all the cards. We can wait."

"You mean that?" Marcel asked.

155

"Yes. Go on in the house and start getting our crap together. All of you. Move. All right, Papa," he raised his voice. "You win this round. But you can't take back the sections of land you done give us over the years. All them acres is ours free and clear. That's ours now and forever."

"Damn," John said for Bull's ears only. "I forgot about that."

"Hell, me, too," Bull said sourly. "I did the same thing while land-grabbin' and snatchin' up everything in sight. Don't look like we'll ever get shut of them."

"Get gone," John told his kids.

"You're gonna have to move me," Utah Bates said. Then his hands twitched.

John shot him. The rancher's draw was deceptively swift for a man his size and age. Utah had cleared leather, but just barely before the slug struck him square in the center of the chest and knocked him flat on his back.

"Oh, hell!" the young would-be tough yelled. His boots drummed the hard-packed earth, and then he was still.

Johnny and Clement Carlin stared at their father. They all knew their dad was quick with a short gun, but they had never dreamed he was this quick.

Pete and Petunia stared in shock.

"Anybody else?" John questioned, his words hard as the man himself.

A couple of the younger ones wanted to try him, but they wisely kept their hands still.

"Throw that dead coyote across his saddle and tie

him in place," John told those few still facing him. "Get him off my property and bury him away from here."

Some of the other older gunslingers were already riding out. They did not wave or look back. John's children were still standing on the front porch.

"You best rattle your hocks," John warned them.

"We're takin' our share of the cattle!" Marcel blurted.

John faced him. "You're takin' nothin', boy. You got no share of my herds." He tapped his pocket, breast high. "I just changed my will. All legal and proper. You get nothin'. Nothin' at all. Now, or ever. Now get your connivin' butts off my property and don't never set foot back here again. Your names will be stricken from the family Bible and from this moment on, you are no kin of mine. Go suck up to Miles Singer."

That shocked the Carlin kids. "How did you . . . ?" Petunia bit back the words as Pete clenched his fists so tightly the knuckles whitened.

"How ain't important," her father told her. "But we know."

J.B. Adams and Ben Connors slowed their horses, and J.B. said to Matt, "You're responsible for all this, Bodine. I'll bet my boots and saddle on that. We'll be around. We'll meet up sooner or later."

"You won't be betting your boots and saddle, J.B.," Matt told him.

"Huh?"

"You'll be betting your life."

J.B. snorted and rode on. Yok Zapata reined up.

"You'll face me first, Bodine."

"I'll take you, Yok," Sam said. "I can't let my brother have all the fun."

"I'll be lookin' forward to that." Yok rode on.

Phillip Bacque, Dick Yandle, and Raul Melendez were the next to ride out. They all grinned at Matt and Sam, clear warnings behind the hard smiles.

Paul Stewart, Simon Green, and Dick Laurin were the next to go. "I got a bullet with your name on it, Breed," Paul said to Sam.

"Keep dreaming," Sam told him.

Simon and Dick smiled at Matt, Simon saying, "I'm gonna kill you, Bodine."

"You'll have to get in line," Matt responded.

Will Jennings, Jack Norman, and Bill Lowry rode by. Jack gave Matt an obscene gesture, and Matt returned it.

"That's a new one on me," Parley said. "I've never seen that before. What's it mean?"

Matt told him, and the young deputy blushed.

Big Dan Parker, Paul Brown, and Ned Kerry rode out. All three of them had to run their mouths and make their threats. Matt waved at them and smiled.

Henry Rogers, Rod Hansen, and Bob Coody were the next to leave. Bob Coody reined up and stared at Sam. "I hate Injuns," he said.

"You should never hate," Sam told him. "It isn't good for you."

"And I don't like smart alecks, neither," Coody said.

"I am so sorry to hear that," Sam told him. "It must be terrible to hate oneself."

158

"Huh?"

"Never mind. Ride on."

"I think he in-sulted you," Rod said.

"Hell with him," Coody said.

Chuckie and Rambling Ed Clark rode by. "See you around, Bodine," Ramblin' Ed called.

"I hope not," Matt replied.

"Bet on it," Chuckie told him. "You and that goddamn half-breed brother of yourn."

"I'll look forward to meeting you," Sam met the gunfighter's eyes.

"It'll be the last thing you see," Chuckie bragged.

Sam laughed at him.

Petunia drove past in her buggy. She looked at her father and gave him a very profane and lengthy vocal expression of just how she felt about him.

"What a delightfully expressive and demure young lady," Sam remarked.

Petunia heard it and told Sam what he could do to himself.

"That's impossible," Sam said.

"Try it anyway," the young woman told him.

"I'd like to see that," Matt said with a grin.

Burl Golden was the last of the hired guns to leave. He walked his horse up to the group and looked down at them. "It ain't over, John, Bull. You must know that."

The ranchers nodded their heads in agreement. Bull said, "You goin' to work for Miles Singer now?"

Burl shrugged his shoulders. "If the money's right, I reckon so."

"A smart man would ride on out," John told him.

"Some people ranch, others practice the law, still others run stores. I hire my gun. It's what I do." Burl lifted the reins and rode on toward town.

John looked as his sons, carrying carpetbags and bedrolls, left the house and walked toward the corral.

"Yonder goes my life," the rancher said. "It was all going to be theirs. Everything I worked for. How could a man get to my age and still be so damn stupid?"

His wife came out to stand by his side. "I have a suggestion, John."

"I'm sure open to them."

"When this is all over and done with, we'll go to that orphanage north of here and bring back a half dozen children. We're not too old to start over. We both like the sounds of kids in the house."

"You want some company?" Bull asked.

John and Ginny smiled their replies. John said, "You ready to go clean out your nest of varmints, brother?"

"Let's do it," Bull said.

13

The men met Randy Sutton on the road into town. Bull cut his horse in front of his son, halting him. "The rest of your no-count brothers and sisters packin', boy?"

"Yeah." The reply was sullen. "You happy about that, you cheap bastard?"

Bull leaned over and slapped the young man clear out of the saddle. Randy's butt hit the ground, and his hand dropped to the butt of his gun.

"Do it," Bull growled the words. "Just do it, you little turd."

Randy smiled through his bloody lips. "I reckon not. That would be too easy. We got other plans for you."

"I'm sure you do."

Randy got to his feet and brushed the dirt from his jeans. "Do I have your permission to leave now, your great lord and majesty?"

"Why, boy?" Bull asked. "Why you kids did it is all

I want to know."

"Money. What else?"

"But you had everything in the world you ever asked for. What more do you want?"

"To step out of your shadow," the second son replied. "We're all sick of livin' in your shadow."

"Well, you're damn sure clear of it now."

"Suits the hell outta me." He looked at John Carlin. "And you can go to hell, too." Randy stepped into the saddle and rode off without looking back.

"What a sorry day," Bull said, and rode on.

The Sutton kids were all waiting on the front porch for their dad. The girls had not been crying. They were dry-eyed and mean-looking.

"You waiting on a formal invite to carry your butts?" Bull asked them, swinging down from the saddle.

Scarlett gave her father a solid cussing. Bull stood and took it. He knew he had somehow failed his kids, but he wasn't sure exactly how he'd done it. What they were, he figured, he'd had a hand in making them.

Roz stepped out of the house, grabbed her daughter by the shoulder and spun her around. Then she slapped her across the mouth. "You do not speak to your father in such a manner."

Scarlett gave back what she had just received, smacking her mother across the mouth. Connie stepped out onto the boards, balled up a fist and knocked her sister slap off the porch.

Scarlett turned to Wanda and Willa and said, "Either of you want to try me?"

They didn't.

Shorty and Cleat walked up, leading their horses. "We're leavin' with the kids," Shorty announced. "We got time comin'."

Bull threw some money onto the ground. "Take it and clear out."

"We've proved up the land you give us," Hugh said. "You can't run us off of that."

"Oh, I can," Bull said. "But as long as you stay clear of me, I won't. Just don't try to steal my cattle and don't ever come onto my range. Randy said you all wanted to get clear of my shadow. You're clear. You got some land, enough for you all to have nice spreads. Now you'll see what work is. Now you'll see what it's like to fight blizzards and droughts. Now you'll see what it's like to stay in the saddle for twenty-four hours or more at a time, breaking the ice off waterholes and movin' cattle to keep them from freezin' to death. You'll . . . ."

"Aw, hell, shut up!" Hugh shouted at his father. "No one wants to hear your goddamn old stories about how hard you worked. We're sick of hearin' 'em."

"Then hear this," Bull said. He told them about the changing of the will, told them about Miles Singer and how John had fired all the gunfighters. "The war is over."

Scarlett was sitting on the ground in a most unladylike pose, dabbing at her busted mouth with a handkerchief. "That's what you think," she told her pa. "I'll be servin' tea in the sittin' room of this house before this is all over. You just wait and see."

163

"You all have ten minutes to clear out," Bull told his kids. "I suggest you get movin'."

"You gonna make us walk?" Ross asked.

"Take your horses and a spare mount. I closed out my bank account in town and opened a small one for each of you. You'll be able to get by. But you'll have to watch every penny from now on. Don't come squallin' to me when your money runs out."

"I 'spect, Pa," Hugh said, "we'll be lookin' at each other over gun barrels 'fore this is all over."

"I hope not, boy," Bull told him. "I surely hope not."

The Sutton brood got on their horses and into their buggies and pulled out.

Bull turned to John. "What do you say we combine our spreads and call it the Circle B?"

"Sounds good to me," John replied. "But what's the 'B' stand for?"

"Brothers," Bull said.

Book Two

Nothing great will ever be achieved without great men, and men are great only if they are determined to be so.

De Gaulle

1

John ordered the Carlin House closed and told the bartender and the swamper to report for work at the newly named Crossville Saloon. The Bull's Den was just as gone as the Carlin House. Several gunhands went in and bought the old Bull's Den—with money provided by the Carlin and Sutton kids—and renamed it the Red Dog Saloon.

"Not terribly original," Sam had commented.

The Express carried the headlines: "PEACE."

Doc Blaine looked at the thirty-odd gunhands drifting in and out of town, but as yet causing no trouble, and remarked to a patient, "That headline just might be a little premature."

Matt and Sam were staying on at the newly named Circle B, working as cowhands until more punchers could be found. The combined ranges of the two men were huge, the largest in the territory, and they needed a lot of men to work the cattle, ride fences, cut hay for winter feed, and do the many other jobs that working cowboys did.

Matt and Sam had ridden into town with Daniel and two hands driving wagons to pick up supplies, and they reined in at the new bank, The Crossville Cattle Exchange, where Matt and Sam had transferred their holdings from Singer's bank.

Daniel looked up the street and said, "Trouble coming."

Hugh and Randy Sutton, with a half dozen of the mangiest looking men Matt had seen in many a day, were riding slowly up the street.

"Where in the hell did he find that motley crew?" Sam asked, just as Donner, Butch Proctor, and Dud Mackin wandered out of the Red Dog Saloon to stand on the boardwalk. "Right on cue," Sam muttered. "It's a set-up."

"Big doin's 'bout fifteen miles west of here," a cowboy from the AT spread said, walking up. "Tom and all his deputies left about two hours ago. Some sort of shootin', I think it was." He looked north. "Well, now, look there, will you. Something funny goin' on here."

Matt looked. Henry Rogers, Rod Hansen, and Bob Coody were swinging down from their saddles in front of the Mexican cafe at the end of the main street.

"We're boxed," Daniel said softly.

"When the shootin' starts, Daniel," Lars said, "you hit the ground. You're your pa's sole son now. You got to stay alive. And don't argue with me."

"I can hold my own," Daniel protested.

"He's right," Matt told the young man. "Just hit the ground at the first pistol crack."

"Don't argue, boy," Slim said. "Just do it."

"Get the people off the street," Sam said, turning to the AT rider. "All hell's going to break loose here in about two minutes."

The AT man took off in a bow-legged trot.

Sam moved to his horse and took his spare six-gun from a saddlebag.

"Look at the bank," Lars said. "There's Singer standin' in the door."

The big man was smiling as he stood in the open door to his bank.

"There's Miss Petunia and Miss Wanda on the porch of the hotel," Slim said. "Looks like they're gettin' ready to enjoy the show."

"Who knew we were coming into town?" Sam asked, shoving the spare six-gun behind his belt.

"We always come into town on a Wednesday for supplies," Lars said. "The Circle JC in the mornin', Bull's boys in the afternoon. They worked that out a long time ago. It wouldn't take no dictionary maker to set this up."

"Comin' up behind us in the alley," Lars said, cutting his eyes. "I'll handle this bunch. Get ready, it's about to blow up on us."

"Now!" Hugh Sutton screamed, jerking out both guns and blasting away.

Sam tossed Daniel to the ground, behind the water trough, just as the warm air was filled with hot lead.

Lars hauled out a long barreled Peacemaker and shot one of those sneaking up behind the bunch in the belly. His buddies broke and ran for whatever cover they could find. Lars dropped to one knee and nailed another in the leg, sending the man sprawling on his face in the alley.

Sam lined up a bearded fat man who had ridden in with the Sutton boys and drilled him in the brisket, doubling the man over and dropping him on his butt in the street.

Ross Sutton appeared in the doorway of Singer's bank, both hands filled with guns. Matt snapped a shot at him that missed and knocked a chunk of wood from the door frame just as Slim fired and blew Ross's hat off his head. The young man hollered and fell back into the bank.

"Goddamnit!" Singer yelled from the bank. "Get off me, you buffoon!"

Matt turned and gave Henry Rogers a .44 round that caught the gunfighter in the hip and spun him around and knocked him to the boardwalk. Hollering in pain, the man crawled into the darkness of the Red Dog, trailing blood as he went.

"You're worth a thousand dollars to me!" a man dressed in farmer's overalls and low-heeled boots yelled to Sam. He leveled a pistol, and Sam plugged him, just as he squeezed the trigger recognizing the man as the gunslinger called Farmer John. The Farmer took the round in the side and staggered back, tripping on the edge of the boardwalk and falling heavily to the boards, losing his pistol.

Slim got burned on the shoulder and grunted at the sudden pain. Recovering his balance, he shot one of the Sutton gunmen right between the eyes, the man dropping like a rag doll.

Matt faced Rod Hansen, and the two men blasted

away at each other. Matt felt the tug of a bullet on his shirt sleeve and another spat dirt at his boots as Rod was shooting too fast. Matt coolly took aim and put a .44 slug in the center of the hired gun's chest. Rod opened his mouth as his eyes widened in astonishment, and he sat down on the boardwalk, his hands falling to his side, the guns tumbling from them. His head lolled forward, and he died sitting on his butt. Slowly, he fell to one side, resting in death against a support post of the awning.

Bob Coody saw the battle, as lopsided as it was, was going against his bunch and high-tailed his butt into the saloon and ran out the back door, heading for his horse.

Daniel Carlin crawled to a shooting position behind the trough and triggered off a round, the bullet striking one of the Sutton gunfighters in the knee, knocking the man down, hollering in pain all the way to the dirt. He lifted his pistol and managed to jack back the hammer just as Daniel fired again, the slug taking the man in the center of the face.

The Sutton boys had disappeared, leaving the fighting to the men they had hired. The air between the buildings of the main street was filled with gunsmoke and the moaning of the wounded.

Matt and Sam were standing very nearly shoulder to shoulder and taking a dreadful toll on those gunslingers still standing and battling in the street.

Henry Rogers had smashed out a front window of the Red Dog and was blasting away with both guns. Lars turned his guns toward the saloon just as Matt and Sam and Daniel did the same. A thunderous

171

valley of shots tore holes in the front wall, and the hot lead literally shot Henry Rogers into bloody ribbons. He died still gripping his six-guns.

One of the six men hired by the Sutton boys was still alive and standing on his feet, and he quickly sized up the situation as being really lousy and turned and ran into the alley between the general store and Miss Charlotte's Dress Shop.

Sam was bleeding from a scratch on the cheek, made by a flying splinter, Matt had a bullet-burn on his arm, Lars was unhit, and Slim had a burn on his shoulder. Daniel crawled to his boots, dusty but unhurt.

The sounds of galloping horses fading into the distance reached the people who were now stepping cautiously out onto the boardwalk and into the bloody street.

Petunia Carlin and Wanda Sutton had vanished from the front porch of the hotel.

Doc Blaine ran up, carrying his little black bag, the editor of the paper right behind him, carrying his bulky photographic equipment. He quickly set up and began taking pictures of the bloody scene and of the men still standing in front of the Crossville Cattle Exchange Bank.

Willa Sutton suddenly appeared at a second floor window of the hotel and began blasting away with a rifle. The street cleared very quickly as the lead started bouncing around and whining off of this and that.

"You murderin' scum!" she squalled, in a voice that would crack brass.

One of her slugs knocked one of the tripod legs out from under the camera and sent the equipment crashing to the street and Ralph Masters flapping his arms and dashing for cover.

"We'll show this damn two-bit town!" Scarlett Sutton hollered, stepping out onto the front porch of the hotel and leveling a shotgun. She pulled both triggers, and the recoil knocked her through a window and sent her crashing into the lobby. The desk clerk wrestled the shotgun from her and suffered various contusions and abrasions to his person doing so. Not to mention a good cussing from the young lady. The buckshot from the shotgun hurt no one, but it damn sure cleared the street of anyone who had not already exited the area.

"Take your damn hands off my sister!" Wanda Sutton screamed from the stairs and began shooting with a hogleg she pulled from her purse.

None of the girls could hit a barn if they were standing inside it, but they could sure scatter some lead around. The desk clerk went out the same window that Scarlett had come crashing through about a minute before and fell off the porch. He jumped to his feet and rounded the side of the hotel at speeds he hadn't reached since boyhood.

Wanda shot down the chandelier, stopped the grandfather clock permanently at ten past ten, sent the chef crawling under a chopping block, and plugged a couple of sofas and chairs before running out of ammunition.

"Somebody do something about them damn girls!" a citizen hollered from behind the protection of a water-filled fire barrel in an alley.

"Well, hell!" Slim hollered, belly down in the dirt. "You can't shoot a woman."

"I'm not so sure about that," Sam muttered, under the boardwalk.

"I can!" a citizen's wife yelled, and proceeded to blast away at the hotel with a rifle.

"Jesus Christ!" a traveling drummer hollered from behind an overturned table in the dining room. One of her slugs had just punctured the coffee urn, and the large urn was spewing out hot coffee.

The woman's husband managed to get the .44-40 from his wife before she killed somebody.

"We got to ride, girls," Scarlett said. "They'll be warrants out for us after this. Get some britches on, and let's haul our butts outta here."

"Somebody get some guns," Willa suggested.

The townspeople were just coming out of their various hiding places when the girls, Wanda, Willa, Scarlett, and Petunia, stole four saddled mounts and took off out of town, riding straight up the main street. John Carlin and Bull Sutton were riding into town, to tie up some legal business, when they spotted the girls coming hell bent for leather their way. The girls weren't much good with guns, but they could all ride like the wind.

"Yeee-haw!" yelled Willa, firing a pistol into the air.

"Good God!" Bull said, trying to stay in the saddle on his spooked horse.

"Whaa-hoo!" shrieked Petunia, a six-shooter in each hand and the reins in her teeth.

"Holy Christ!" John said, as he went one way off the road and Bull went the other to avoid being run down by their rampaging daughters.

"Get outta the way, goddamnit!" squalled Scarlett.

The ranchers got their horses under control and rode on into town. They reined up at the sight of the bloody and body-littered street.

"Your boy's all right, Bull," a man told the rancher.

"What happened?" Bull asked.

"Well, ah . . ."

"Say it."

"Your other boys tried to bushwhack Daniel and the others in his party. Then the gals shot up the town."

The brothers rode slowly on, John saying, "You know it's goin' to be up to us to put an end to this matter, don't you?"

"I'm afraid you're right, John. But it makes me sick at my stomach to think about it."

"I feel like pukin' right now."

The men stepped down, and Bull walked over to Doc Blaine, as he attended a wounded gunhand. "Farmer John," Bull said. "You should have stayed away from here."

"Mornin', Bull," the gunslinger said cheerfully. "I was gonna call them boys out proper like, but your oldest boy jumped the gun and started bangin' away. He's shore got a powerful hate on for Daniel. Has he got the money to back up his words like he say he do?"

"He's got some money of his own, yeah."

"Then he'll just hire some more ol' boys and not rest until either he's dead or Daniel is."

"You'll live," Doc Blaine told the man.

"You don't sound too happy about that, Doc," Farmer said.

"Should I be?" Doc Blaine said, as he moved to another wounded gunslinger. He knelt down beside the fat man and cut open his shirt. Blaine looked the man in the eyes and shook his head.

The fat man closed his eyes and cussed.

"Now, now, brother," Pastor Fowler said, squatting down. "That is no way to meet your Maker."

The bartender and the swamper dragged the bullet-riddled body of Henry Rogers out of the saloon and dumped it in the street. "Here's another one," the swamper called.

"Oh, my," the undertaker said, rushing from body to body, rubbing his hands together and mentally counting the money he would make. "See if they have any cash on them before we agree to bury them," he called to his helper.

"This one is dead," a man called from near the bank. "Shot right 'tween the eyes."

"I done that," Slim said.

"Pretty good shootin'," Bull complimented him.

"You boys all right?" John said, turning to Matt and Sam.

"Oh, yes," Sam said. "Just a little dusty and a little worse for wear, is all."

"Bull," Matt said. "Can I ask you a question?"

"Whatever you like, Matt."

"When was the last time you took a belt to the behinds of your daughters?"

"I never did except when they were little," he admitted. "But I sure should have."

A dog wandered over to the boardwalk, inspected the body of Rod Hansen, then hiked his leg.

"I can't think of a more apt tribute," Doc Blaine said.

2

The Sutton kids and the Carlin kids just seemed to drop off the face of the earth. A drifting cowboy said he saw a bunch of young people, men and women, camped out northeast of the town, in the rugged mountain country. He said they were real unfriendly, and he didn't tarry long. He said the young folks also had with them about a dozen randy-lookin' gunfighters. The cowboy was hired by John Carlin.

The town of Crossville buried the dead gunslingers without fanfare, patched up the others, and for a week not one shot was heard. Repairs were made to the hotel, and the chef bought himself a double-barreled, sawed-off shotgun to keep in the kitchen, just in case the Carlin and Sutton girls decided to make another appearance.

John Carlin now had hired enough punchers to maintain his herds, and Matt and Sam waved away his offer of payment for their services. Ginny Carlin and Roz Sutton had become close friends and often visited one another. They immediately became active in county affairs and began organizing drives to aid the less fortunate with clothing and food and so forth.

"A happy ending," Sam opined.

"You believe that?" Matt asked him.

"No. But it sounds good."

"Let's go pay Ladue a visit," Matt suggested. "Check out his general mood."

Ladue was about as friendly as a rattlesnake with its tail caught in a beaver trap.

"If you two hadn't a stuck your noses into affairs that don't concern you," the surly old mountain man grumbled, "all this mess would have been settled."

"You encouraged us to stay," Sam reminded him.

"I was lookin' forward to a good gunfight, and you two gettin' kilt."

Matt sat down without being asked and said, "You think it all belongs to you, right?"

Ladue's eyes narrowed, the slits showing a lot of mean. "Bright boy, ain't you? Goddamn right, it's mine. I was here first. So that makes it mine."

"I believe the Indians were here first," Sam corrected. "So if you apply that logic, it belongs to them. Right?"

Ladue chose not to respond to that.

"Who told Bull Sutton that John Carlin stole his initial herds?" Matt asked.

Ladue mumbled something under his breath.

"He only had about four hundred head when he first came out here," Sam said. "Just about the same size herd as Bull. And he's still got the papers to prove he bought them in Illinois and Missouri."

"Come on, Ladue," Matt pressed. "Level with us. You know the Carlin and Sutton kids aren't going to win this fight. The territorial governor will order militia in here if he has to. What's your real stake in all this?"

The old man smiled, sort of like a weasel in a full henhouse. "You boys think you're so smart, you figure it out. Now git out of my tradin' post and don't come back."

On the ride back to town, Sam said, "Could Ladue be the real father of Carlin and Sutton and Singer?"

"I don't think so. He doesn't fit the description the men have of their father. I think he's just a bitter old man who would like to see things like they were thirty-five or forty years ago."

"Of course, we have yet to talk to Singer," Sam reminded him.

"Want to try again?"

Singer stared at the two men and finally waved them to his office and into chairs. The bank was void of customers, and Singer had no employees left. The tellers had gone to work over at the Cattle Exchange Bank.

"I certainly have no reason to be friendly toward you," the man admitted openly. "I just about had it all until you two showed up." He smiled, but it was not a pretty sight. "And I might yet. Now then, what do you want? As if I couldn't make a reasonably accurate guess."

"Why all the hate toward your half brothers?" Sam asked.

181

"I don't hate them," Singer said, a surprised look on his face. "This is just business for me. And I'm only a half brother to John. Bull and I are full brothers."

"Your father?"

"Oh, he's dead. He was a reprobate and a rake, but a wealthy one. He left me pretty well fixed back East. A jealous husband finally shot the old bastard years ago."

"Ladue?"

"He's my uncle. My father's brother. He is also as crazy as a loon. Father said he was always strange, but the mountains drove him over the edge. I had no idea he was still alive. But I recognized him from an old tintype my father had in his possession."

Matt stared at the man for a moment. "And now you're bank-rolling the kids in their fight against their fathers?"

Singer smiled. "Now you don't expect me to admit to anything like that, do you?"

"It was worth a try."

"Anything else, boys?"

"You're plotting to kill your own brother and your own half brother, and you have no more feeling about it than shooting a rattlesnake," Sam said, leaning forward. "What the hell kind of person are you?"

"I'm not plotting to kill anybody," Singer said with another smile. "Those are your words. I'm looking at this from a purely business standpoint. If something unfortunate happens to my brothers, well, I would be truly sorry about that and would make my best offer to buy their ranches. And I would be most generous, I assure you. Now, then, boys, since I fully expect you both to run tattling to John and Bull with every word I just said, I have taken the precaution of hiring several bodyguards. They came in yesterday. Two of them are standing behind you right now."

Matt and Sam turned. "Hello, Matt," a tall, cold-eyed man said, no smile accompanying his greeting.

"Hello, Donner," Matt said. "Who's your buddy?"

"Nyeburn. You have heard the name, I'm sure."

"I've seen it written on the inside of outhouse walls from time to time, yeah."

Nyeburn tensed and Singer said, "Hold your peace, boys. The time will come. Chase Martin and Blue Anderson are outside, Matt. I believe you're both familiar with those names, too."

"We've heard them," Sam said, pushing back his chair and standing up. He smiled at Singer as Matt got to his feet. "You didn't pull top gunslingers in here for John and Bull, Singer. You pulled them in for us. So that makes it real personal."

"You're just scarin' me to death, Sam," Nyeburn said with a sneering smile. "The day I back up from some goddamn half-breed Injun will be the day I . . ."

He never got to finish it. Sam spun around and wiped the sneer off his face with a solid right fist to the mouth. Nyeburn's boots flew out from under him, and he landed heavily, his mouth a bloody smear. He started crawling slowly to his boots just as Sam reached down, jerked Nyeburn's Colt from leather, and tossed it to the floor.

Donner had turned around at the blow, dropping his hand to the butt of his pistol, and he suddenly felt the cold muzzle of a .44 against his neck. "We'll just keep this honest, backshooter," Matt said, jacking back the hammer. "If any of your people outside try to interfere, you're a dead man."

"You're buyin' yourself a lot of grief, Bodine," the hired gun said.

"I'm just scared to death, Donnor. Shut up."

The two bodyguards outside came rushing in and to a fast halt when they saw the .44 pressed against Donnor's neck.

"Just stand back and enjoy the show, boys," Matt told them. "It'll be a good one, I can promise you that."

Nyeburn lurched to his boots and lifted his fists. "You sucker punched me, breed," he told Sam. "Now I'm gonna beat your head in."

"I doubt it," Sam replied, and kicked the man on the knee cap.

Nyeburn hollered and stumbled back, the pain in his knee sending bright lights flashing through his head. The lights obscured Sam's moving forward and busting the man twice, one blow to the mouth, the other to the nose. Nyeburn's nose was pushed to one side, and the fractured olfactory squirted blood.

"Fight fair," Chase hollered.

"Get out of my bank!" Singer yelled. "You'll get blood all over everything."

Nyeburn stumbled away from the wall and took a wild swing at Sam. Sam sidestepped, stuck out his boot, tripping the man, and Nyeburn fell against a depositor's table and went crashing to the floor.

Tom Riley and his deputies had appeared on the boardwalk, all of them smiling at the scene.

"Do something, Marshal!" Singer shouted. "They're going to wreck my bank."

"Who started this?" Tom called over the sounds of confusion and falling furniture.

"Nyeburn's big mouth," Matt told him. Tom shrugged.

Nyeburn climbed slowly to his boots, his eyes burning wild with hate. He cussed Sam as the blood from his busted beak ran down his lower jaw.

Sam waited patiently, his hands balled into gloved fists.

Nyeburn rushed Sam, his arms folding around Sam's legs and both of them went propelling backward, crashing through a big front window of the bank.

"By God, you'll pay for that!" Singer shouted.

Amid a shower of broken glass, both men struggled to their feet and faced each other. Nyeburn got in a good lick to Sam's jaw that backed him up, and Nyeburn, sensing early victory, pressed in. Bad mistake.

Sam planted his boots and gave Nyeburn two shots to the head, a left and right to the jaw that staggered the man and sent him stumbling back. By now, everybody inside the bank had moved outside, and Tom's deputies were covering the three bodyguards, the three of them knowing that should they try to interfere with the beating their buddy was taking, the

185

odds were pretty good that would be the last thing they would ever do. They stood grim-faced and watched Sam Two Wolves stomp Nyeburn.

Nyeburn stepped up and flicked a left to Sam's face. Sam brushed it off and didn't fall for the fake. Nyeburn tried again, and Sam blasted a right through the opening that caught Nyeburn flush in the mouth and knocked him down, flat on his back on the boardwalk.

Sam stepped back and waited.

Nyeburn was not so quick getting to his feet this time around. He staggered once, caught himself, and looked around him for his buddies. He saw they were effectively blocked from doing anything other than watching. "Now I'll finish this once and for all," Nyeburn said with an added curse, then reached behind him and came up with a knife. Tom stepped quickly out of the crowd, just behind the gunfighter, and laid a heavy cosh against the man's head. Nyeburn dropped unconscious to the boardwalk.

"I'll put up with a fistfight for a time," the marshal said. "But not when it gets down to this." He reached down and picked up the long-bladed knife. "Sharp," he remarked, running a finger carefully over the blade. "All right, boys. Drag him over to the jail and let him cool off."

"What about my busted up bank and the broken windows?" Singer yelled.

"Fix it yourself," Tom told him shortly. "Or better yet, why don't you board it up and leave town? That way you'd make everybody around here happy."

Sputtering with anger, Singer stepped back into

his bank and slammed the front door hard. The glass popped out of it and went crashing to the boardwalk.

The men sat on the front porch of John Carlin's ranchhouse and listened to Matt and Sam relate the events of the day.

"So Miles Singer is my full brother," Bull said softly. "The youngest of the three boys."

"Three boys that we know of," John added. "And that old mountain man Ladue is our uncle. Life sure takes some funny twists and turns as it moves us toward the grave."

"That's almost poetry, John," his wife said with a smile.

John ducked his head to hide his embarrassment.

Bull sipped his strong coffee and was silent for a moment. "Singer never wears a gun, so we can't call him out. I'm sure that's deliberate on his part. He's hired bodyguards that, I'm equally sure, will probably shoot either one of us or both of us on sight if the right moment ever comes along. Our kids, including the girls, are on the dodge, living in the mountains with a pack of outlaws and ne'er-do-wells, all of them ready to put a bullet in us at any time. I have been in some sorry situations in my life, but none to compare with this. Getting drunk doesn't help. I know, I tried that."

"Let's see if my addition is right," John said. "There are still about twenty gunhands hangin' around, right? Gunslingers that I brought in . . ."

"Or hired from me," Bull stepped in, glancing at

187

him. "We both have to share equally in that stupid move."

"I count nineteen," Sam said.

"That's about as close to twenty as you can get, boy," John said, smiling at him.

"But that's not counting the four that Singer imported in," Matt said. "And the bunch that lined up in the mountains with your kids."

"You said you were going to get in touch with the territorial governor," Matt said, looking at Bull. "What did he say?"

"He said, and I quote, 'There hasn't been enough provocation for him to warrant sending in the state militia.' In other words, he's hoping we'll all kill each other off. He doesn't like me or John and has never made any bones about that."

"Of course, we haven't given him much reason in the past to like us," John was forced to admit.

"You're sure right there," Bull agreed.

One of the newly hired hands came riding in, turned his horse into the corral, and walked over to the porch. "Boss, I seen sign that a whole bunch of riders have moved onto our range. They come in from the mountains."

"Comin' which way?" Bull asked.

The puncher thought about that for a moment. "Hard to tell, Mr. Bull. The lot of them fell in behind a bunch of cattle movin' toward water. But the way the cattle was movin' was direct to here."

Bull and John rose as one. "They're going to try here first," Bull said.

John turned to the puncher. "Tell the boys to get

188

their guns loaded up and ready for a fight. We're gonna be outnumbered.''

"We'll be ready, boss,'' the cowboy assured him, then took off at a trot for the bunkhouse.

"It's a hell of a thing to say at this late date,'' Bull said. "But despite all my big talk, I don't know if I can let a hammer fall on my own flesh and blood.''

"Sir?'' Sam said, looking at the Bull in the fading light of day. "You wouldn't be much of a man if it came easy to you.''

3

The women were told to go into the house, but neither John nor Bull made the mistake of telling them to stay down low and out of trouble. These were frontier women, and they might have told their husbands—in a ladylike manner, of course—where to stick that suggestion.

Ginny and Roz were upstairs, sitting by a window, each with a Winchester rifle. Connie was at the side of the house, also upstairs, with a long barreled ten-gauge goose gun, loaded up with buckshot. At the range she would be shooting from the bedroom window, she could do terrible damage with the big goose gun, and she definitely knew how to use it.

"Rider comin'!" the shout came from the barn.

"Damn fools," John said. "Don't they know that the advantage is ours because we hold the high and protected ground?"

"They're riding with hate guiding them, John." Bull spoke out of the darkness.

"What if the girls are with them?" John asked, a sick note to his voice.

"I thought about that," Sam said. "I got a couple of punchers ready over there in those trees . . . with ropes."

"I bet they'll be sorry when they drop a loop over one of those gals," Matt said. "Sorry, Bull, John."

"No need for sorry when you're right," Bull told him. "I hope they do jerk my girls out of the saddle. When I get through working on their fannies, I think they'll have a brand new outlook on life."

"The boys?" Sam questioned.

Bull hesitated. The pounding of hooves grew louder. "I honestly don't know," he replied, and then there was no more time for talk.

The area around the house and barn and bunkhouse filled with what seemed to be fifty or more riders, although all knew it was not that many. The dust made anything hard to see. Connie drew first blood. A duster-clad and hooded man carrying a flaming torch burst out of the dust and drew back his arm to throw the torch through a window of the house. Connie sighted him in and blew him clean out of the saddle.

There wasn't a whole lot left of his upper torso when he hit the ground. The powder load pushing buckshot very nearly tore him in two.

Matt lined up a rider just as Bull lined up the same one. Both men fired, and the rider threw up his arms, his pistol sailing away, and he hit the ground and did not move.

"Get this rope off of me, you no-good son of a . . ."

192

The pounding hooves obscured Scarlett's last few words.

"You are in deep road apples, girl," Bull said through clenched teeth.

"I busted my ass!" Petunia squalled over the sounds of battle and galloping horses.

"Not nearly as bad as I'm goin' to," John muttered.

Ginny Carlin led a galloping rider and squeezed the trigger. The .44-.40 slug knocked him out of the saddle and rolling on the ground. Roz Sutton broke the shoulder of another night rider and put him out of action for a time.

A rider very stupidly tried to ride onto the porch, and John stood up, reversed his Winchester and gave the outlaw the butt of the rifle smack in his teeth. The mask flew from his lower face and pearlies went sailing all over the place. The rider dropped from the saddle to the porch, unconscious and in need of false teeth.

"Bastard," John said.

The first wave of the ill-conceived attack was broken, and the night riders cleared out, at least for the time being. The daughters of John Carlin and Bull Sutton were brought kicking and biting and scratching and cussing up to the porch.

"I think I'll go help with the wounded," Sam said.

"Me, too," Matt echoed.

Each father had a big hard hand clamped down tight on the back of a young lady's neck, the men's wide leather belts were already removed and dangling from the other hand.

"I'm gone!" the two punchers who had brought the girls to the porch said in unison.

"You bastard! You're not gonna hit me with that . . . WHOOOEEE!" Scarlett hollered as the leather impacted with tight jeans.

"You miserable son of a . . . OUUCCHHHH!" Petunia bellered as the whapping sound drifted out across the dust-covered front yard.

"DADDY!" Scarlett bellered. "WHOOOOEE!"

"PAPA!" Petunia shrieked as the leather popped again.

"In the house!" Bull said, and the leather cracked again, and Scarlett jumped and hollered.

"Move, girl!" John yelled, and the belt came down hard, and Petunia whooped and bellered her outrage, her indignation, and her pain.

The cowboy, Batty, put his hands to the rear of his jeans and grimaced at just the thought.

About five minutes passed, during which time the butts of the young ladies were thoroughly blistered by angry fathers swinging wide leather belts. The sobbing girls were then handed over to their mothers. If Petunia and Scarlett expected a velvet hand to comfort them in their time of need, they were sorely (in more ways than one) disappointed.

"WHOOOEEE, MAMA!" Scarlett let out a shriek. "I'll be good, Mama. I promise."

"WOWEEE, MAMA!" Petunia bellered, as a belt was applied to her backside. "I'll be a lady, Mama. I'll be good. I swear I will!"

A shot from out in the darkness slammed into the wall of the bunkhouse and sent everybody scurrying for cover.

"We can wait you out," a voice called. "It might be a week before anybody from town come out to check on you."

"He's right about that last bit," John said, from his position behind the stone railing on the front porch. "But wrong about everything else. Come the dawn we can spot them and flush them out. I thinned the trees and cleared the rocks and filled in the gullies around this place years ago to prevent just such a thing from happenin'. Just keep your heads down. It's goin' to be a long night, boys."

The ladies, after seeing to it that Petunia and Scarlett were in no condition to run away (the girls would be sleeping on their stomachs and doing precious little sitting down for several days), went to the kitchen, located in the center of the house and well protected, and helped the cook fix plenty of strong coffee and lots of sandwiches. The men in the bunkhouse had their own fixin's for coffee and sandwiches and could safely relay them to those in the barn.

The defenders of the grounds settled in for a long wait through the night's darkness.

All except for Matt and Sam. "We're going to do some head-hunting," Sam told the ranchers. "Don't worry. We were both schooled in this beginning way back when we were no more than babies."

"I believe it," Bull said, knowing the fierceness of the Cheyenne warrior and suspecting rightly that both Matt and Sam had been initiated into the Cheyenne Dog Soldier society.

195

The blood-bonded brothers took off their boots and spurs and slipped into moccasins. They left their rifles and took only pistols and knives. Within seconds, they were lost from view, moving as silent stalking ghosts through the occasionally gunshot-punctured night.

Sam drew first blood. He moved up behind a duster-clad night rider and left him sprawled in his own blood, his throat cut from ear to ear. Sam waited by the dead man, knowing that Matt would be on his target within seconds, if he wasn't already there and doing the deed.

"Oh, my, God!" the call reached Sam. "They done got amongst us. They done sliced Hal's throat wide open. They's blood ever'-where."

Matt, like Sam, waited motionlessly on the ground, not fifteen feet from the man who had shouted out the frightful warning.

Matt used to kid Sam about the tomahawk he carried in his saddlebags. But Matt knew the war axe, in the hands of someone who had been trained to use it, was a fearsome weapon, and Sam was well-schooled in this particular method of killing. Matt was no slouch at it, either.

A man that Sam had seen around town over the past week or so reared up a few yards from him. Sam waited. The man slowly looked all around him, attempting to see through the murkiness. When his back was fully toward him, and the man paused for a moment, Sam flung the war axe with deadly accuracy. The head embedded in the man's skull, and he threw out his arms and fell to the ground without making a sound.

Matt had heard the dull smacking sound and knew his brother had cut the odds down by one more.

"Ace!" the almost panicked whisper came from Sam's right. "Ace. Answer me, boy. Where is you at?"

Assuming that the man you are hailing is the one now with a war axe in his head, Sam thought, lying motionlessly on the ground, he is probably in Hell.

"Anybody seen Petunia or my sister Scarlett?" the mule-voiced Wanda brayed into the night. No way in hell could she manage a whisper.

And the voice came from no more than a few yards away from where Matt had slipped.

Oh, Lord! he thought. Please, don't let me have to put up with taking her prisoner this night.

"Them down yonder put a rope around both of them," a man said. "I seen 'em jerked out of the saddle."

"Damn," Wanda said, and moved on her hands and knees directly toward Matt.

Matt tensed and silently cursed. This was no time for a struggle of any sort. If the girl came up on him, he would have to pop her on the jaw and hope for the best. But he did not want to hit a woman. Even Wanda or Willa.

Well, not too hard anyway.

"Maybe they got away," Wanda said. "I'm gonna circle around and check."

"You be careful," Hugh called, but he was some distance away.

"Yeah, yeah," Wanda said, and crawled right up nose to nose with Matt.

Sam's eyes had adjusted to the night, and he could see what was happening below him on the ridge. He had to inwardly struggle to keep from laughing.

Wanda's eyes widened in fright and shock, and she opened her mouth to let out a squall when Matt's fist caught her on the side of the jaw. Wanda dropped like a rock.

"What was that?" the question was flung out from below Matt.

"I didn't hear nothin' a-tall. You're imaginin' things, Billy."

Matt got to his knees and, trying hard not to grunt, managed to get Wanda across his shoulders. The young woman was no light-weight. She certainly hadn't missed a meal since being born. And to make matters worse, she needed a bath really bad.

Sam made sure his brother had a clear path to the top of the ridge by taking out the last sentry in that area and then suddenly appearing at Matt's side in the night. Matt had been expecting him and was only a tad startled. "You bringing in an early Christmas gift, brother? What do you have there, a calf?"

"Very funny," Matt returned the whisper. "This heifer is not petite, to say the least. We'd better not go back the same way we came up."

"Agreed. The creek is our best shot. I'll work point. But for God's sake, keep that one quiet. If she starts braying, we're dead."

"You want her?"

"Thank you, no. I had a pet cougar one time. Once was quite enough."

Once off the ridge and close to the creek, the

brothers had to stop and stuff a bandanna into Wanda's mouth to keep her from squalling and bellering, then they had to stop again to truss her up tight with their belts to keep her from scratching and kicking. Matt had dropped her unceremoniously on the ground, knocking the wind from her.

"I hope my pants don't fall off," Sam bitched.

Wanda kicked out with both tied boots, and Sam narrowly missed getting his bell rung.

"Girl," Sam warned. "You are beginning to try my patience."

Behind her gag she mumbled something terribly profane. Matt hoisted her to his shoulder with a grunt, and they started along the creek. They left the creek and called out to the rear of the bunkhouse.

"Matt and Sam, coming in with Wanda."

"Better you than me," Lars said.

The brothers slipped through the darkness and made the front porch. "I got another one for you, Bull," Matt said, dumping the bound girl on the porch. "Good luck."

"I don't know whether to thank you or hit you," the rancher replied.

Matt backed up.

Bull reached down and jerked the girl to her boots. He sniffed once and wrinkled his nose. "Damn, girl. Have you gone on strike against bathing?"

She fought her bounds and tried to push words past the gag in her mouth. It was a good thing her father couldn't make out all the words. The few that he heard were quite enough.

"This is the strangest situation I have ever been

in," Sam whispered to Matt, as both of them knelt at a far end of the porch, behind the rock railing. "We are surrounded by people wanting very much to kill us, and the fathers of the girls are ignoring that fact and concentrating on dealing out punishment to their daughters. I don't know why I ever let you talk me into this."

Matt ignored that last bit, knowing that a dynamite charge couldn't drive Sam away from this private family war. He was just as curious as Matt to see the outcome.

"We have a skunk on our hands, Mother," Bull called into the darkened house. The lamp lights from the kitchen could not be seen on the outside. "Fix up lots of hot water so's we can get the stink off of her."

Wanda muttered curses and tried to kick her father, and that got her a pretty good pop on the jaw from a big, work-hardened palm. The blow stilled her muffled, profane mumblings and brought tears to her eyes. Bull reached up and tore the gag from her.

"You get popped everytime you cuss me or yell out to your no-count brothers and friends," he told her. "You understand that?"

Wanda understood it. She stood with her hands at her sides and her mouth closed. For a change.

"Now get on inside the house and take a bath," her father told her. "You can wear some of Petunia's clothes she left behind. You don't sass me or your mother; you don't cuss me or your mother; you don't do nothin' except what we tell you to do. Your days of runnin' high and wide are over, and you'd damn well better understand it. Do you?"

"Yes, Papa," she said humbly.

Bull opened the door, and she walked in with him right behind her, followed by John Carlin. In the kitchen, she joined her sister and Petunia. Both of them were scrubbed clean and wearing dresses and very subdued.

While the bath water was heating, John asked, "What made you kids think you could get away with this wild scheme?"

"Our brothers," Wanda and Petunia said together. Scarlett nodded her head in agreement.

"The boys hate us that much?" Bull asked, his tone gentle but firm.

"Yes, Papa," Scarlett said. "You probably won't believe this, but at first none of us girls wanted anything to do with their plans. I won't pretend to excuse what we did by laying all the blame on them, but they had to work on us for a time before we agreed to go along with them. But only after they agreed that you and Mama wouldn't be hurt."

Neither Bull nor John believed all that she'd said, but neither of them wanted to give up entirely on their daughters. Still, they didn't trust them any further than they could see them. These girls were schemers and connivers. But maybe not as vicious as their brothers. Time alone would tell that. But neither man held out much hope.

The girls all started babbling about how sorry they were and how it would never happen again and to please forgive them and how much they loved their mamas and papas and so forth and so on. The husbands looked at their wives and saw that the women didn't believe a word they were hearing from their offspring. It was a depressingly bad act. The tears were put-on, and the eyes of the girls were evil and hard. The parents let their turncoat kids run down, and the room fell silent.

"Take your bath and get upstairs with Petunia and Scarlett," Bull told the girl. "Don't try to run. We're all operatin' on a short fuse and trigger fingers are itchy this night."

The men walked through the darkened house and stood for a moment in the room that led to the porch.

"You believe anything they said?" John asked.

"No," Bull said, a weary note in his voice. "I don't trust any of them. But I'll give them one more chance. Even a mean dog deserves that."

"And when they turn on us again?"

"I hoped you wouldn't ask that." Bull pushed open the screen door and stepped out onto the porch, picking up his rifle. He turned to his half brother. "'Cause I damn sure don't know the answer."

4

The gang left their dead where they lay and pulled out sometime during the night. The ranch hands dragged the bodies in and buried them in unmarked graves. No one knew any name to put on the markers. The rider with the busted jaw and no front teeth was trussed up and handed over to Tom Riley and his deputies. He refused to say who he was working for or where the gang was hiding out.

"They'll have changed hideouts by this time," Matt said. "Probably outside of this county."

"I'd bet they're south of us," John said. "Just across the line in Utah."

"Can you prove it was your boys?" Tom asked both men.

Bull shook his head, "Not unless the girls swear statements. You can ask them."

Tom did and the girls all said their brothers had planned the raid but did not come along. The girls said they just came along for the adventure of it. They

203

didn't think anyone would be hurt, and surely no one would be killed. It was just a hoo-rahin', that was all. Surely the marshal didn't think they would take part in doin' harm to their parents?

"Lyin' little no-good's," John said, his big hands balled into fists, anger ready to boil to the surface.

"You heard at least one of our kids out yonder, didn't you, boys?" Bull asked Matt and Sam.

"Hugh," Matt replied. "But I didn't see him."

"You boys stay here with John, if you don't mind," Bull said. "I've got more hands than John, and a couple of them are as salty as any who ever sat a saddle. Tom brought me word that I've got four more men in town. Cowboys, not gunfighters. But they know how to use guns. John's more shook up over this situation than I am. He's still undecided, but I know what I'm going to do." Without adding anything to that, he swung into the saddle and fell in behind his wife and their errant daughters, the girls sitting in the bed of a wagon, on lots of hay. They all glared hate at the blood brothers.

"I wonder what he's got in his head to do?" Matt asked.

"Finish it," Sam said. "I'll make a wager he's going to take the fight to them this time."

"And he's telling us to stay out of it."

"That's the message I got."

"You boys don't have to stay here," John said, walking up. "But there is something you can do for me, if you will."

"Name it."

"Escort Petunia into town and put her on the

afternoon stage. She says she doesn't want to rejoin her brothers and damned if she'll stay here with her mother and me. Says she wants to go to New York City and become an actress. Both her mother and me said that was just fine with us." He took off his hat and rubbed his forehead. "I...," he verbally stumbled for a second, "... think this will be the last time her mother and me will ever see her. I view that with mixed emotions, but mostly with relief."

"John," Matt said. "Sure, we'll escort her into town. But there's something else. Your boys and Bull's boys are going to brace me and Sam one of these days. Probably pretty damn quick. I just want you to know..."

John waved him silent. "You do what you have to do, Matt, Sam. You're dealing with renegades now. Night-riding outlaws. They came here last night to kill me, their mother, their brother, and anyone else who happened to be here. So don't hesitate on my account. Bull thinks I haven't made up my mind. But he's very wrong. You boys ride easy, now. And you're always welcome out here. No matter what happens."

After John had walked away, Matt said, "I think they both got their heads together and planned something. But they don't want us in on it. They plan to stomp on their own snakes."

"A hard thing for them, but I'm glad we won't be a part of it."

"I wonder if we'll be that lucky."

Petunia never said a word on the way into town. She sat on a pillow in the buggy seat and stared straight ahead. Only when they reached town did she speak.

"I suppose my father asked you gentlemen to personally see that I got on the stage?"

"Yes," Sam told her. "He did. You have some objections to that?"

"Not a one. Just don't touch me." She smiled at both brothers, but it was a savage smile. "My brothers will kill you both. My only regret is that I won't be here to see you crawling in your own blood."

"You are really a charming young lady," Matt said.

"Thank you. I wondered when you would realize that obvious fact."

For two whole days the town of Crossville was quiet and free of trouble. The same bunch of hired guns drifted in and out, but they caused no ruckus of any kind.

Miles Singer had closed his bank and in its place had opened a land office. The four gunslingers he'd hired as bodyguards hung around and loafed, trailing and fronting him wherever he went.

The town seemed peaceful enough, but all its residents could detect a slight air of tension. Sort of like when the fellow in the hotel room above yours drops one boot on the floor and never drops the other one. You keep waiting.

Matt and Sam watched as Batty came fogging into town, waved at them, and then jumped out of the saddle and rushed into the marshal's office. He came out, waved, and called, "I need me a beer. Talk to you two in a minute."

"You boys hang around and help Parley if he needs it," Tom said, exiting his office and walking up to them, buckling on his gunbelt. "John and Bull lost about five hundred head of cattle last night, apiece."

"Next thing you know, they'll be hirin' regulators," Matt opined.

"Not in this county," Tom straightened that out real quick. "I'll shoot a damn back-shootin' regulator as quick as I will a rustler. And I already told Bull and John that, long before you two come wanderin' into this Godawful mess. I'll see you boys later on. I imagine it'll be a couple of days 'fore we get back."

The brothers watched as the marshal, his deputies, and a ten man posse, all heavily armed and with several days' rations, rode out.

"Some of the most able-bodied men and best shots in town," Sam observed.

Matt looked up and down the street as young Parley joined them on the boardwalk. The smithy had closed up and gone with the posse, as had the man from the saddle and gun shop. The tough young man who ran the livery had gone. The barber, who was a seasoned veteran of the Indian wars had closed up and ridden out. The Mexican, who had fought Apaches and Comanches down south and who ran the cafe, had gone, leaving his wife and daughter to run the business.

"There is an interesting look on your face, Mr.

Bodine," Ralph Masters said, joining the group. "Anything I can write about?"

"I hope not," Matt replied mysteriously. And that got him a sharp look from Sam.

The editor wandered on up the boardwalk. "What's on your mind, Matt?" Sam asked.

"Same thing that's on yours."

"With some of the best shots in town gone for several days, this would be a dandy time for the Sutton-Carlin boys to hit us."

"Exactly."

"You think stealin' those cattle was a trick?" Parley asked.

"I wouldn't be surprised. Now let's keep our eyes open and watch for gunslingers to start drifting into town. If a lot of them show up, that would be a pretty good sign that something is up."

"Parley, you'd better tell the men you know will stand to load up their guns and keep them handy," Sam said. "You take the other side, and Matt and I will work this side of the street."

"There aren't that many left," the young deputy said.

"Yeah," Matt said softly. "We know."

Batty had stayed in town after hearing the news, saying, "They's plenty of hands at the ranch to fight off any attack should that happen. But I think you're right. I think right here is where it's gonna pop."

"Farmer John's up and around," Parley said. "I

208

seen him standing in the Red Dog, and he's wearin' two guns."

Doc Blaine walked up, and the men were surprised to see that he was wearing a gunbelt, a second six-shooter shoved behind the belt. He smiled at their startled glances. "I only said I didn't like guns, boys. I didn't say there wasn't a need for them or that I couldn't use one."

"There's Shorty and Cleat ridin' in," Batty said. "And a couple with them I ain't seen before."

"That's the first time they've come to town since they quit Mr. Bull," Parley said. "Or at least the first time I've seen them in town."

"Look at the south end of town," Matt said. "There come Dud, Proctor, and Donner."

"There's Coody stepping out of the livery," Sam pointed out. "Two men right behind him."

"Only a couple of real gunhands," Matt said. "Makes me wonder where the others are."

"They're close by," Doc Blaine said. "We can all bet on that."

The men stood silent for a few moments, watching. "The bank!" Matt spoke the words hard. "That's what they want. If they could clean out the bank, they'll have this town on the ropes, along with Bull and John, 'cause it's their money that started it. Then they'd start rustling all of their cattle and wipe them out. You asked where the other top guns are, Doc? Probably about a mile out on either side of town. When the shooting starts, they'll come in fast and hit the bank and the stores, cleaning them out of cash. If they could manage that, this town would die, or at best, be so crippled it might not ever recover."

"If that's true," Doc Blaine said, "somebody planned this very carefully. But I can't believe it was any of the Carlin or Sutton kids. None of them are that smart."

"The man who planned it is standing right over there in the doorway to his land office," Sam said. "Miles Singer."

"Why don't we just plug the skunk now and be done with it?" Batty suggested.

"It's a nice thought," Doc said. "But he's unarmed. As usual. He's a careful man. It would be out and out murder. Sorry, Batty."

"But it was a good thought," Sam surprised Matt by saying. Of the two blood brothers, Sam had a tad more respect for law than did his brother. And that was odd when one took into consideration that the law almost never treated Indians with the same respect and due process as it did whites.

"Interesting thing for you to say," Matt said.

"I do have my moments when frustration builds to the boiling point," Sam replied drily.

"You sure do talk funny," Batty said.

A young boy walked out of the alley and up to the men. He had a .22 caliber single shot rifle and carried two fat rabbits hooked onto his belt. "Deputy," he said, "I seen a whole bunch of really crummy lookin' men over by the crick east of us. They told me if I said anything about them, they'd skin me alive. I told them to go to hell and took off runnin'."

210

Parley laughed and said, "You did just fine, Billy. Now you go on home and take care of your mother. And don't leave the house, now, you hear me? It's gonna get real dangerous out here in a minute."

The lad lifted his rifle. "Any of those bad ones come close to me and Ma, they're gonna get plugged."

"That sounds good, Billy, but don't take any chances. Now, go on home. Hurry!"

The boy took off at a run, his dog yapping right beside him.

"Hey, Cleat!" Shorty hollered, stepping out onto the boardwalk in front of the Red Dog. "I betcha a dollar I can hit that runnin' mutt from here."

"You're on," Cleat hollered.

Billy heard every word, stopped, and knelt down, rage on his face. He leveled his little .22 and let it bang.

He was just a tad off his aim. The little slug, instead of hitting Cleat between the eyes, tore off part of the man's ear. Cleat howled and dropped his six-gun. "Shoot that goddamn kid, Shorty!" Cleat screamed, the blood pouring down the side of his face.

Shorty jerked iron and leveled his .45 at Billy, frantically trying to reload and protect his dog at the same time.

Four six-guns roared from across the street, and Shorty was slammed back by a barrage of .44 and .45 slugs. He fell through the newly installed front window of the saloon and did not move.

"I'll kill that goddamn punk kid!" Cleat yelled, and clawed for his other gun.

He never made it. Doc Blaine drilled him clean from a good eighty-five paces away. "Anybody who would shoot an innocent dog is a sorry enough excuse for a human being," Doc said, lowering his pistol. "But anybody who would shoot a child is on a level with snake crap."

Cleat managed to get up on one elbow, cock and lift his pistol, and Doc plugged him again. He did not move after that. It would have been a miracle if he had, for Doc's second round took him in the center of the forehead.

Singer stood in the doorway, stunned by the doctor's shooting of the man. His bodyguards all looked at one another, as if they didn't know what to do next.

Farmer John's bulk filled the half-pushed open batwings of the saloon. He, too, had a quizzical look on his face.

Coody and his two buddies stood by the broken window of the Red Dog, along with Les and Willie.

"Get the hell home, Billy!" Parley shouted. "Like right now, damnit."

Billy got.

Doc quickly reloaded and stepped back into a store stoop.

"Back," Matt urged his friends. "Take cover."

"What the hell are they waiting for?" Batty asked, backing up and kneeling down behind a quickly overturned bench.

"Here they come!" a shopowner shouted from the

roof of his store. "My God, there must be forty of them."

Parley had returned to the marshal's office for sawed-off shotguns and bags of shells. He passed them around.

"This is not going to be pleasant," Sam said.

He was right.

5

Unknown to Matt and Sam and Deputy Parley Davis, a few of the ladies of the town had met secretly during the last few days and formed their own plans as to the protection of life and property. Armed with rifles, shotguns, and various types of pistols, including a few Dragoons, the ladies took their positions inside the Crossville Cattle Exchange Bank, the general store, the dress shop, and a few other businesses. The outlaws who had foolishly decided to attack and loot and attempt to destroy this Western town were going to be in for the shock of their lives. And for some of them, it was going to be a very brief shock . . . the last thing they would know on this earth.

An outlaw known ony as Chub kicked in the back door to Miss Charlotte's Dress Shop and stomped in, both hands filled with guns. "Git over there agin that damn wall!" he ordered the ladies. "After I see what's in the money box, I'll pleasure myself with a couple of you. So you might as well strip and save me the trouble of rippin' them rags offen you."

Mrs. Hortense Pennypacker told the unwashed lout what he could do with his orders, and where he could stick them. Before the startled outlaw could reply, Mrs. Pennypacker lifted a double-barreled shotgun and blew Chub slap out the back door.

Miss Charlotte picked up the outlaw's guns from where he had dropped them from lifeless fingers and checked the loads. Full. She smiled grimly and moved to the front of the store. "Courage, ladies," she said. "Decency and justice will prevail and sustain us through this ordeal." She lifted both pistols and fired through the show window just as one group of the outlaws began their wild, screaming charge up the main street. The .45 slugs knocked an outlaw off his horse and put him dead in the dust.

Matt and Sam lined up a racing rider and fired as one. The outlaw threw up both hands and tumbled from the saddle. One boot twisted and hung in the stirrup, and the man was dragged to the point of being unrecognizable to the edge of town, across the bridge, and beyond.

Singer was quick to realize that his plan was not going to work. "Get back in here!" he told his bodyguards. "It's going sour. Move. Quickly!"

"It just started!" Neyburn protested, stepping into the land office.

"Nobody trees a Western town," Blue said, coming in right behind him. "I told ever'body concerned it wouldn't work."

"Stop bickering," Singer shushed them over the rattle of gunfire. "Let's just keep our heads down.

There is always tomorrow."

"Not for them boys out yonder," Donner said bitterly, his eyes on the dust-churned street.

Doc Blaine was standing inside the dubious protection of the entrance to the barber shop, choosing his targets carefully and firing with deadly accuracy.

A wild-eyed outlaw who had been thrown from his frightened horse, and sensing that things were not going well for his side, ran up the alley in a panic and burst into the rear of Wo Fong's laundry. Wo Fong was waiting by the door. Wo very forcefully laid a heavy iron to the side of the man's head, and the outlaw dropped to the floor, his head busted open and his skull fractured. Wo Fong carefully barred the back door to his shop, picked up the dying man's guns, and moved to the front of his establishment, muttering dark curses in his native tongue. Wo Fong wasn't all that familiar with a six-shooter, but he'd seen other men use them, and figured he could, too.

Les and Willie ran from the rear of the Mexican Cafe, across the alley, and onto the boardwalk by the edge of Wo Fong's. Wo turned at the sound, lifted both .45s, and started blasting through the window.

Wo didn't do much damage, but he sure scared the pee out of the two young gunhands as he let the lead fly just as fast as he could cock and pull the trigger. Les got his hat blowed off, and Willie lost the bootheel on his left boot, the impact of the .45 slug bending his spur and driving part of it through the leather and into his foot. It knocked him down and brought a shriek of fright from the man, sure he had lost his foot.

Wo started yelling in Chinese, and that only made matters worse for the gunmen, both of them now certain they were under attack from hordes of wild-eyed foreign savages.

Les and Willie took off for the protection of the creek bank, Les minus his new hat and Willie limping badly.

Wo Fong returned to the dying outlaw, took off his gunbelt and reloaded. He slung the belt around his narrow hips and stood ready to repel any other intruders.

Paul Mitchell and Bobby Dumas ran onto the back porch of the pastor's residence by the church. Bad move. William and Melinda Fowler had reached their limit of patience when it came to lawlessness. Paul opened the back door, and the reverend shot him with a load of birdshot, the lead taking him in the chest and belly. The light loads didn't do a whole lot of permanent damage, but they damn sure ruined Paul's day. Certain he was mortally wounded, the gunhand howled in pain and spun around, his chest and belly bloody. He ran over Bobby and knocked the man off the porch just as Melinda stepped out and tossed a pot of hot coffee on Bobby, the scalding liquid splashing on Bobby's back and the side of his face. Shrieking in more pain that his buddy was enduring, Bobby joined Paul in running away.

William reloaded and let fire another load of birdshot. Most of it missed but for the rest of his life, Bobby would carry lead in his ass.

"Bastards!" William muttered.

Sour-faced Lawyer Sprague had taken his rifle and moved to a window of his second floor office. A combat-hardened veteran of the War Between the States, Sprague was methodically choosing his targets and dropping a man with each round fired. The lawyer despised lawlessness, and despite his chosen profession, had absolutely no sympathy for those who chose the outlaw trail. "Contemptible scum," he said.

Farmer John, after seeing very quickly that the attack was doomed to failure, got him a bottle and a glass and retired to the darkness of a far corner of the saloon. "Bloody day," the hired gun muttered as he filled a glass. "But none of my blood is gonna be spilt."

Most of the older and wiser guns-for-hire felt the same way, and they stayed out of this attack.

"Stay down!" Bob Coody told the two men with him. "It's a deathtrap out yonder."

"We're tryin' the bank," they told him.

"You're damn fools if you do."

"Hell with you." The two ran across the dust-filled street and up the alley, heading for the rear of the bank.

"Idiots," Bob said, and headed for the livery and his horse. He was getting gone from this town for this day. But he passed by the house where young Billy was protecting his ma and his puppy. Billy lined him up and pulled the trigger. The .22 slug slammed into Coody's gunbelt and discharged several .45 caliber rounds. Coody did a wild dance as he tried to both run and rip off his exploding gunbelt. Billy put another slug into Coody's thigh, and the man yelled and pitched forward into the murky safety of the cavernous livery. "Jesus!" Coody said, limping toward his horse. "What fool dreamed up this plan?" He saddled up and got out of there.

The two who decided to try the bank slammed open the back door and charged in. They had only a few seconds to realize the error of their decision. Four shotguns roared, and the two were slung back outside, one dead before he hit the ground and the other badly wounded.

The dust from frightened, rampaging and riderless horses was thick in the air, and the gunsmoke was arid, hanging close in the streets. But the battle was very nearly over . . . at least this round of it.

Matt and Sam cautiously looked around for any of the known gunhands. But few of them had ever even shown up for this disaster, perhaps sensing that is what it would turn into. They might be paid gunmen and in some cases cold-blooded killers, but that did not make them stupid. Just a little short in the morals department.

A hired gun staggered out of an alley and screamed curses at Matt and Sam. He lifted an empty hand and tried to cock the pistol that wasn't there. "Damn you!" he shouted hoarsely. "Damn you both to the hellfires." Then he collapsed face-down in the street.

"Do you know that fellow?" Sam asked.

"I never saw him before in my life," Matt replied, punching out empties and reloading.

"Name is Barton," Parley said. "He's a drifter and a no-good. When he does work, he works for Ladue."

"It's beginning to get a bit clearer now," Sam said.

Doc Blaine had holstered his pistols and was now carrying his black bag. The undertaker and his helper were wandering from body to body, the helper carrying a tape measure and jotting down measurements.

Farmer John had left the saloon and was standing on the boardwalk, sipping at a glass of whiskey. Dud, Proctor, and Donner joined him. They stood silently, looking at the carnage that lay still and bloody in the street. Only a few who had attempted to tree the town were still alive.

"They's four back here in this alley," a shout came. "One is still breathin'."

"Wo Fong's got one in his cleanin' place," a woman hollered. "He busted his head with an iron."

"Two behind the bank," a man yelled.

"One behind Miss Charlotte's," a woman called.

Matt and Sam and Parley walked the street and the alleys, looking at the dead and wounded. They stopped in front of Singer's Land Office and looked in through the open door. The four bodyguards were sitting in the outer office, Singer sitting alone in his big office.

"It didn't work out quite like you planned, did it, Singer?" Matt called.

Ralph Masters' flashpan popped. The newspaperman was busy taking pictures of the dead. Somebody had propped Chub up on a board with his rifle in his dead hands and was charging two bits to anyone who wanted to pose for a picture.

Miss Charlotte had kept Chub's pistols.

"Somebody get that one the horse dragged," Parley ordered. "Toss him in a wagon and bring him back here."

"Eighteen dead and four still breathin', Parley," a citizen reported. "I ain't never seen nothin' like this."

"I hope I never see anything like it again," the young deputy replied.

"You will," Lawyer Sprague said, walking up, still carrying his rifle. "The worst is yet to come." He looked in on Singer. "Isn't that right, Singer?"

"I don't know what you're talking about!" Singer said hotly. "This is a terrible, terrible thing that happened to this lovely town today. A tragedy, I say. I have never before witnessed such an overt act of wanton brutishness. I . . ."

"Oh, blow it out your backflap, you big windbag," the lawyer said, and walked on up the street.

"You'd better leave town while you're still able," Sam told Singer. "I think your time is growing rather short."

Singer glared at him and said nothing.

Parley walked across the street, and the blood-bonded brothers walked on. They climbed the stairs to the hotel, which had not received a single bullet hole this time around, and went into the dining room.

"Coffee," Matt said, just as the chef stuck his head out of the kitchen. Matt started laughing. The chef wore a Prussian-style helmet complete with high plume.

He frowned at the brothers and disappeared back into the safety of his kitchen.

Sam wiped his eyes and said, "The way things are going, that helmet is not such a bad idea."

Matt stared at him for a moment, working up a mental picture of Sam in a Prussian helmet, and busted out laughing again.

Sam did his best to look hurt. "I think I would appear quite dashing."

"Oh, I do, too, Sam. I do, too."

One of the badly wounded gunmen still lying in the dirt of the street lifted himself up on one elbow and took a shot at young Parley. The shot missed the deputy, busted one of the front windows of the dining room, and shattered the vase of flowers on the table where Matt and Sam were sitting. Both men hit the floor. The bullet stopped when it impacted against the brand new coffee urn. It now had a hole in it, spewing hot coffee. The chef hollered as he hit the floor of the kitchen, cussing in French and German.

The gunman shook his head at his bad marksmanship and then lost consciousness, the six-gun slipping from his hand.

Sam looked at Matt, both of them under the table. He pointed a finger at his blood brother. "I told you weeks ago that we should have headed south. But no, you wanted to see the Idaho Territory."

"You didn't have to come along, you know."

"I promised your parents I'd look after you."

The men crawled out from under the table and moved to another table, this one a bit more protected. They stopped at the coffee urn and held their cups under the stream of coffee gushing from the urn, filling them full.

"You got any pie?" Matt hollered, seating himself at the table.

"The kitchen is closed!" the chef shouted.

"Look there," Sam said, cutting his eyes. "Someone is getting desperate."

A lone rider was walking his horse up the street. The man was dressed all in black, from his hat to his polished boots, and carried his rifle across his saddle horn. Even at this distance Matt recognized the rider.

"Gates," Matt said.

The chef came out of the kitchen with two huge wedges of apple pie. "I changed my mind," he explained. "The shooting wasn't the fault of you gentlemen. And the pie is delicious." Then he picked up on the direction his only customers' eyes were taking. "Who is that?"

"Wilbur Gates," Sam said. "Nobody really knows where he's from. But he's a long-distance shooter. And I've never known him to miss."

The chef tossed the plates of pie on the table and beat it back to his kitchen. He was still wearing his helmet.

"I wonder who brought him in and who he's after?" Matt asked.

"Killing us would solve nothing," Sam said. "We're not the principal players in this little drama. But that isn't to say Gates wouldn't shoot us if we got in his way."

Matt knew that was a pure fact. "Sam? Is there a fifth player in all this mess?"

Sam stared at him for a few seconds. "Why would you think that?"

Matt forked him a piece of pie and chewed for a moment. Gates had swung down from his horse and walked into the Red Dog, carrying his deadly rifle. He was not a big man, but that rifle made him a giant. "Who slipped that note under our door?"

"I've thought about that. I've given it a lot of thought. I don't know. There isn't anyone else in town who stands to gain by all this."

"There has to be. Nothing else figures. Think about it. Who in town—what businessman—is making money out of all this? Who stands to profit by keeping all this stirred up? John and Bull can be discounted. The Sutton and Carlin kids don't have the sense to plan something this complex. Singer is devious, but as far as I'm concerned, he's just about played out his string. So there has to be someone else."

"Not Ladue?"

"No. Ladue is a half-crazy, bitter old man."

"I'm stumped."

"So am I."

"Well, a good lunch will give us time to ponder it."

"God, Sam, you're eatin' half a pie, now!"

"You're forgetting your Cheyenne upbringing."

"Please, spare me that."

"I should never have rescued you that day. But then, we all make mistakes." Sam ducked his head to hide his smile.

"You, rescued me? I seem to recall it was me who dug you out from under that dead pony when we were kids."

"That was merely a ruse on my part. I was tricking you, that's all. I could have gotten out anytime. I was going to take your scalp."

Matt leaned back in his chair and laughed at that. Sam had never taken a scalp in his life. The very idea of it disgusted him. Besides, as Sam pointed out, scalping was a white man's idea in the first place. They brought that practice to the Indians. "You would have died had I not come along. You and the pony would have become as one. Dead. You were one scared little Indian."

"Bah. I have never known fear. Eat," Sam said, waving a fork at Matt's pie plate. "Don't try to think. You know it gives you a headache."

Waiters were busy cleaning up the mess made by the wandering bullet.

Matt looked up the street and suddenly smiled. "I know who the fifth party is."

"So tell me."

"You're so smart, you figure it out."

"All right. I shall. Over a steak. Medium. With potatoes and a side order of scrambled eggs."

"For lunch?"

"Why not?"

"I can see it now. When you're fifty years old you'll have a new name: Big Fat Man Who Makes The Ground Tremble."

The brothers needled each other through lunch. And a second dessert for both of them.

6

A tired posse rode in the next day, Bull and John with them. The men needed only one look at the boarded up windows and the blood stains on the boardwalks to know that one hell of a battle had taken place.

Over coffee, Matt and Sam explained what had taken place.

"And none of our people got hurt?" Tom said. "That's incredible."

"Not a scratch."

"Did you see any of our kids taking part in the fight?" Bull asked.

"No," Sam told the man. "Not a sign of them. But Wilbur Gates is in town."

The marshal slowly took off his hat and then threw it violently to the floor. He cussed softly but with a great deal of expression. He wound down and said, "I'm going to get a bite to eat, then sleep for a few hours. Then . . ."

"There's more," Matt said.

Tom looked at him.

"Ralph Masters is keeping all this stirred up."

"What?"

"Has to be. He's making a small fortune selling this story and the accompanying pictures to the big city papers back East. He's got to be the one who slipped that note under our door. He's not in any conspiracy with Singer or any . . ." Matt paused, a reflective look on his face.

"What's the matter?" Sam asked.

"Think back, Sam. After the Carlin and Sutton kids staged that mock battle and tried to kill John, remember I told you that I saw Singer looking at me sort of funny?"

"Yeah. And you also said you thought somebody was with him in his offices. Who was it?"

"Ladue."

Sam and Tom and the deputies all looked at Matt, Parley finally saying, "You know, you may be right. I saw old Ladue that day, ridin' out of town with somebody. I don't remember who it was."

"Which way were they heading?" John said, a grim note to his words.

"Toward the crick where you and Mr. Sutton was gonna meet."

"I hate this. I helped Ralph get set up here," John said with a frown.

"Hell, so did I," Bull said.

"What?" John stared at his half brother. "He told me that he felt you were entirely in the wrong and I was in the right."

"He told me that I was in the right, and you were in

228

the wrong."

"That lyin' little weasel! The damn little no-count played both ends against the middle, and we never caught on."

"This is givin' me a headache," Tom said, his fingertips rubbing his temples. "But something doesn't figure. Look, what has Ralph Masters got to gain from all this? As soon as it's over, it'll be old news."

"He and Ladue just might be playing a very dangerous game," Sam said, after a moment's thought. "This situation here is fraught with deceit and back-stabbing. We might not have to do anything except light the fuse and stand back and watch it blow up in everybody's face."

All the men looked around at each other, all of them deep in thought. "I'm thinkin' right along the same lines you are, boy," Bull said. "But let's just make damn sure that we're not too close when it does blow up."

"What do you two have in mind?" Tom asked.

"Nothing firm yet," Sam said. "At least I don't. We might not have to do anything. It might ignite all by itself. I'm thinking it probably will. Let's just wait and be very cautious while we do so. And keep an eye on Ralph Masters and Miles Singer."

"I'd like to go stomp Singer slap into the damn ground," Bull growled.

"I'd like to go slap the pee out of Masters," John said. "Lyin' little skunk."

"I'd like to jerk up Ladue and shake the truth out of the old fart," Tom said.

Sam smiled and held up a hand. "Patience, gentlemen. Patience."

"I'd give some thought to grabbing up Ladue," Matt said. "That old man would as soon kill you as look at you. He's not playin' with a full deck."

"You can bet your boots and saddle on that," Van Dixon said. "And he ain't got no use for either of you men," he reminded the ranchers.

"There goes Wilbur Gates ridin' out," Nate said, staring out the window. "That is one man who gives me the creeps. I guess I've heard too much about him."

"And none of it good," Matt added.

"Not one word of it," the deputy agreed.

Bull looked at John. "I just wonder which of us Gates has come to kill?"

"It might not be either one of you," Matt said. "This web is so tangled, it could be anybody. Or nobody."

"What do you mean by that?" Tom asked.

"None of us considered that the man just might be passing through."

"Well, you can forget that," Nate said, still staring out the window. "Gates just pulled up at the hotel, and he's gettin' his warbag. Looks like he's here for a spell."

Van picked up the large stack of wanted flyers. Tom cut his eyes and said, "Forget it, Van. Gates is not in there. There are no flyers out on him. I've been behind a badge for more years than I care to think about, and I ain't never seen a wanted poster on Wilbur Gates. He comes into an area, somebody dies,

230

and he leaves without a black mark on him. Nobody has ever been able to prove anything against him."

"What about the cattle that were rustled?" Sam asked.

"Oh, we found them," John said. "'Bout fifteen miles from home range. It was a trick to get the men out of town. Tracks went ever' which-away. We decided to give it up and come on back in."

"What do you want me and John to do, Tom?" Bull asked.

"Stay close to home, and if you just have to do any ridin', don't do it without men with you," the marshal was quick to reply.

"We'll stick to Gates like glue," Matt said, looking at and receiving a nod from Sam. "If he doesn't like it, he can damn well turn and make a play."

"Our kids have to be runnin' out of money," John said. "I know what those gunhands are paid a month. Me and Bull put a crimp in Singer when we pulled out of his bank. He's doin' all he can to pay those high-priced bodyguards of his. I know damn well that Ralph Masters doesn't have that kind of money. Ladue now is another story. That old coot has probably got wads stashed back. And he's got the patience of a cigar store Injun. Damnit!" he almost shouted the word. "I wish I knew what was really goin' on around here."

"It has to come to a head 'fore long," Bull said. "After this attack on the town failed, they all got to be gettin' desperate. And when people reach that point, they get careless. Everybody on all sides. But you and me, John, we just have to make sure that we don't get careless. Not with that back-shootin' Gates in the area. We'll send some boys in with wagons and double stock up with supplies. Then we'll hole up at our ranches. Agreed?"

"Yeah, but it goes against the grain," John said. "I don't like for other people to fight my battles." He looked square at Tom Riley. "Why don't you take a vacation, Tom?"

"And it will all be taken care of when I get back, right, John?"

"You can damn well bet on that."

Tom shook his head. "You know better than even to suggest that, John."

"It was worth a try." He stood up. "I'll be gettin' on."

"Van, you ride with John," Tom said. "Nate, you ride with Bull. You boys take it easy and relax and lay low." He smiled. "Make plans for the big weddin' comin' up."

The ranchers allowed themselves a small smile. "There sure is that," Bull said.

Wilbur Gates took the following for less than one day. On the afternoon of the day after he rode into town, he stopped his horse and turned in the road to face Matt and Sam, not a hundred yards behind him.

"Bodine," the long-distance shooter said, his words hard and cold. "I don't like people following me. Get off my tail and do it now."

"Or you'll do what?" Matt challenged.

Gates' smile was thin. "I'm no fast gun, Bodine."

"No. You're just a back-shootin', cowardly, son-of-a-bitch," Matt said bluntly.

Gates tensed in the saddle but kept his composure. He was wearing a pistol, as did most men, but he knew he was no match for Matt Bodine or Sam Two Wolves. Few men were. Carbone, Monte Carson, Louis Longmont, Charlie Starr, Vonny Dodge, Luke Nations . . . those men, yes. But had any of those men been here, they would be lined up solidly with Bodine and Two Wolves.

"You'll pay for those words, Bodine," the back-shooter said, his voice hoarse.

The two young men faced the long-distance shooter. Sam said, "Ride out of here, Gates. Pack your kit and ride on. If you stay around here, you're going to be buried here."

"Strong words, Two Wolves."

"But true ones."

Gates stared at them for a few seconds. "What's your interest in this? I'm curious about that. You both own ranches. It's rumored that you both have some money. You're not being paid by any faction that I know of. Why are you here?"

"That's an interesting rifle you have there," Matt said. "What is it?"

Gates smiled. "Just a plain ol' .44-.40. Nothing unique about it."

"Somehow I doubt that," Sam said.

"You've been warned, boys," Gates said, his smile gone. "Don't crowd me anymore."

"Oh, we'll be around, Gates," Matt assured him. "Just look over your shoulder, and you'll see us. I can promise you, we're not going to let you out of our sight."

"You two are in no danger."

"But our friends are," Sam said.

Gates wore a puzzled look on his face. "The ranchers? But they are in no danger, either. I may be many things that you abhor, but a liar is not one of them."

Both Matt and Sam knew that to be true. Most paid killers operated under a strange code of conduct. Some would kill a woman but not a child. Others looked with contempt upon those who would steal. Many would have nothing to do with a rapist. Still others would not tell a lie. Gates fell in the last category.

Matt shifted in the saddle and the leather creaked. "Who the hell are you after, Gates?"

"No one who is a friend of yours."

"That doesn't tell us much."

"It's all you need to know if you think about it. Back off, boys. I won't warn you again."

He lifted the reins and deliberately put his back to the brothers. They let him get several hundred yards away and then followed. They followed him all the rest of that afternoon and then back into town. If the man in black was angry, it didn't show in the way he sat his saddle.

He stabled his horse and carrying his rifle, walked the two short blocks to the hotel, Matt and Sam right behind him. He got his key from the desk clerk and ordered bath water sent to his room and told the clerk that he would be having his supper in his room that evening. Halfway up the stairs, he turned and smiled at the blood brothers.

"I hope you enjoyed your ride, boys. I certainly did. I'm sorry we won't be able to do it again. But I'm leaving in the morning. My work here is through."

Matt and Sam turned at the sounds of boots on the lobby floor. Tom Riley. "Ralph Masters is dead, boys. Killed about an hour ago. Shot in the head at close range while he was walking from the privy back to his office. Blew his head off."

Both brothers blinked in shock. Sam found his voice first. "Well, don't blame it on Gates. He was never out of our sight all day."

"I was afraid you were going to say that." Tom hitched at his gunbelt. "Damnit!"

"But when we talked to him this afternoon, he told us he was not here to harm any friend of ours," Matt said. "And you know how he is about lying."

"And he said just seconds ago that he would be leaving in the morning. His work was finished," Sam added.

"What work?" Tom demanded.

"To distract the law while someone else pulled the trigger," Sam suggested.

Tom lost some of his tenseness and anger and sighed. "Yeah. You're probably right. I didn't think about that. Well, I reckon Gates is free to ramble if that's what he's got in mind. I sure can't hold him on anything."

Tom turned to one side to cough and that saved his life. A bullet tore through his shoulder and knocked the man to the floor. Had he not turned when he did, the bullet would have torn through his throat.

"Get Doc Blaine!" Matt yelled, as he and Sam took off for the front door.

"The shot came from the east side," Sam called over his shoulder. "You want the front or the back?"

"You circle around, Sam. I'll take the front. You be careful."

Just before he rounded the corner and stepped into the murk of early evening's twilight, darkened even further by the bulk of the hotel, Matt saw Doc Blaine and the deputies coming at a run. "Van! Somebody cover the bridge and the southeast side of the road. Sam and I will take the rest of it."

"Gotcha, Matt!"

Sam's six-gun roared, and the fire was returned. "They're heading your way, Matt. Two of them. Both of them have rifles."

A slug slammed into the hotel behind Matt, and he snapped a shot at the muzzle blast. A scream followed that, then low curses.

"We got them!" Van yelled. "They can't get away. One's down and the other is headin' your way, Sam."

Sam's pistol roared and silence followed that. "Two down," Sam's voice came out of the gathering gloom.

"Get some men over here!" the desk clerk shouted from the porch. "Carry Tom to Doc's clinic."

"I never saw this one before," Sam said, striking a match and squatting down.

A rifle boomed, and the match went out.

"Sam!" Matt yelled.

"He's hit, Matt!" Van yelled. "Sam's down!"

7

Matt ran through the twilight and jumped down the embankment, sliding down to Sam's side. Van looked up and smiled.

"He's gonna be all right, Matt. The bullet ricocheted off a rock and hit Sam in the side. He's got some busted ribs, but he ain't shot."

Before Matt could respond, a volley of shots split the night. "That's number three," George the bartender's voice came through clear.

"God," another man spoke. "We all must have hit him. He's shot to pieces."

"I'm afraid I'm going to be incapacitated for a time," Sam pushed the words through clenched teeth. "I knew when I struck that match I was making a terrible mistake."

"Shut up," Matt told him. "And hold still." As gently as he could, Matt's fingers moved up to his brother's side. "At least two ribs cracked, maybe three."

"Feels like all of them," Sam groused.

"Wait 'til we try to move you," Matt said. "Then you'll really know it."

"You're such a comfort to me. Go see if you recognize any of the dead."

The dead were dragged and carried to the porch of the hotel, and there, under the eyes of travelers, Matt looked at them. He didn't recognize any of them.

"Russ House," Wilbur Gates said, squatting down beside a body. "That one over there is called Pat. I don't recall ever seeing the third one." He thought for a moment. "Marshal Riley was wearing a black hat and a black shirt this evening. From a distance we resemble slightly. This is interesting."

"You mean they may have been gunning for you and shot Tom by mistake?"

"That is a distinct possibility."

"To shut your mouth as to who hired you to come here and do whatever the hell it is you did?"

Wilbur smiled. "Your words, Bodine. Not mine." He stood up and walked back into the hotel.

Matt left the porch and walked up the street, right behind the men who were carrying the stretcher with Sam.

"Tom's all right," Parley said, as Matt stepped up onto the boardwalk in front of Doc Blaine's little clinic. "The slug punched right through the meaty part of his shoulder. Tom's a tough old bird. The gunmen?"

"All dead. Wilbur Gates identified two of them. He says he didn't know the third one. And he also thinks the snipers may have been after him. Tom was

238

wearing a black hat and black shirt, remember?"

"This thing is gettin' spooky, Matt."

"Yeah. At least that."

The desk clerk came up the street at a flat lope the next morning, waving his arms and shouting for the law. Matt was having coffee with the deputies, and all of them stepped outside at the commotion.

"Whoa, man!" Van calmed the excited desk clerk. "Slow down and tell me what's wrong."

"Wilbur Gates is dead! That's what's wrong. His throat is cut from ear to ear, and there is blood all over the place. The mattress is ruined and so is the carpet. Now, I can't have any more of this, Van. It's bad for business."

"It ain't good for people's health, either," the deputy drawled. "Come on. Let's take a look."

"Razor," Matt said, looking down at the pale face of Wilbur Gates. His eyes were wide open in shocked death. "Or a very, very sharp knife."

"Just look at this room!" the desk clerk said.

"Gather up all his possibles, Parley," Van said. "Tote them over to the office so's I can go through them."

"I'll check his horse and saddle," Matt said, looking around the room. "His rifle's gone."

A search of Gates' possessions turned up nothing. Matt went over the saddle and saddlebags carefully. Nothing. Wilbur Gates would carry his dark secrets to the grave.

Ralph Masters was buried that afternoon, and the

three gunmen were planted without fanfare in the rapidly growing town's Boot Hill. After checking on Sam and Tom Riley, Matt got the key from Van and opened up the newspaper office. He sat until dusk at the desk, going over papers that yielded him nothing except a case of eye strain and a headache.

He went to the Mexican cafe for supper. Raul Melendez was there, drinking tequila and looking grim. Matt almost backed out, then said to hell with it and went on in. A man was playing a guitar and softly singing Spanish love songs.

"Shut up," Raul told the guitarist. "Your singing makes me want to puke."

"I like it," Matt said. "Please continue."

The guitarist stopped playing. He looked at one gunfighter, then the other. He shook his head, picked up his guitar, and left the room.

Raul smiled nastily. "He fears me more than you, gringo."

"Oh, I doubt it," Matt said. "He just made a wise choice, that's all. He probably doesn't want to see you humiliated, that's all."

"I think I will kill you, Bodine," Melendez stated harshly. "I will shoot you to bloody pieces."

"You won't kill me," Matt said calmly, after chewing a mouthful of food. He washed that down with a swallow of beer. He ate and drank with his left hand. His right hand remained close to the butt of his gun. Melendez was not only fast, but he was very tricky.

"Oh, yes, I will. Then I will be the most famous gunfighter in all the West. But I will be gracious

240

about it," the Mexican gunfighter said with a wide smile. "I will allow you time to finish your meal."

"Oh, that's big of you, Raul," Matt replied.

They were alone in the room, all the other patrons having quickly exited, including the owner, the cook and the two waitresses.

Melendez looked around, a frown on his face.

"What's the matter, Raul? Can't you work without an audience?"

Matt saw the man's eyes shift and then swiftly return to him. A very quick smile passed his lips. "I am going to enjoy killing you, Bodine."

Bodine sensed another gunslick had moved in behind him. "I didn't know you were this yellow, Raul."

"What do you mean?" Raul spat out the words.

"You have to have a backshooter behind me?"

Raul smiled. "Very good, Bodine. Come over here, Dud. But Bodine is mine."

Dud Mackin moved to stand beside the seated Mexican gunhand. "I'm gonna enjoy seein' you dead on the floor, Bodine. You're a meddlin' pain in the butt."

Matt smiled and then suddenly jumped up, screaming like a panther. He overturned the table with his left hand, sending dishes and glasses breaking to the floor, and drawing with his right hand. The move was so totally unexpected it shocked both the hired guns, which is exactly what Matt intended. His .44 barked, and Raul Melendez took a round in his left shoulder, knocking him backward.

Matt drew his left hand .44 and drilled Mackin in

the belly, doubling the man over. Then Bodine jumped to one side and dropped to the floor, on his knees, just as Melendez fired.

His slug slammed harmlessly into the wall and for a moment, he and Bodine exchanged shots, both of them on the floor, behind overturned heavy tables. Bodine shot out the hanging lamps above the dining area and plunged the battleground into darkness.

"Oh, God, I'm hard-hit, Raul," Dud gasped. "Kill him for me. Kill him."

Matt quickly loaded up full and waited, not wanting to be the first to fire and give away his position in the darkness. The breathing of the wounded men was loud in the closed space.

Matt felt around him on the floor and picked up an unbroken coffee cup. He hurled it across the room, and it shattered against a wall.

Raul chuckled painfully. "I will not fall for that old trick, Bodine."

Matt put six fast rounds in the direction of the voice and then shifted locations and reloaded as quietly as he could.

There were shouts outside, but no one attempted to enter the darkened cantina. These were Western men and women, and they knew that those inside would fire at the slightest sound or movement.

Dud Mackin staggered to his feet, and Matt shot him, the slug stumbling him backward. Dud fell against a wall and slid down to the floor, on his butt. "Damn you to hell, Bodine," he gasped out the words. "Damn you!"

Matt waited.

"Come on, Bodine," Melendez said. "Come on."

Matt holstered his guns and picked up a chair and threw it with all his might. He must have hit the Mexican squarely in the face for the impact brought a scream of pain. Matt chose that time to move. He stood up as he saw the darkened shape of Melendez rise to his feet, the cane-bottomed chair all tangled up in one arm. Matt emptied his .44 into the man. Raul jerked and staggered and did a strange death-dance with each slug that ripped into his body. He finally fell forward, still tangled up in the chair.

Matt moved to the door and looked out. "Van, Parley?"

"We're here," Van replied. "Nate's over with the marshal. Who's down?"

"Dud Mackin and Raul Melendez. Get some light in here."

Lamps found and lit, Doc Blaine rushed in and knelt down beside the Mexican. He said, "The man's shot to pieces, and he's still alive."

"Bodine," Raul whispered.

Matt squatted down beside him.

"I have money to pay for the damages we caused this poor cafe owner this night. See that he gets it, will you, amigo?"

"I'll see he gets it."

"You are ver' good, Matt Bodine. You are tricky, like me. I always said that when I go out, I want to go out at the hand of someone like you." His bloody lips parted in a smile, and he died.

"Help me, Doc!" Mackin cried out. "Give me something for the pain."

"Wait a minute or so," Doc Blaine said shortly. "You won't have any pain."

"I hate you, Bodine," Dud said. "Shoulda kept your nose out of things that don't concern you. Hadn't been for you and that damn breed brother of yourn, things would have worked out." He coughed up blood. "But it ain't over. Not by a long shot. I hope you . . . I hope you . . ."

Whatever it was he hoped for died with him.

Matt stood up. "I never did get to finish my supper," he said.

Sam griped and moaned about having to stay in bed, but it was all for show. He knew better than to try to get up until his ribs began healing properly. A broke-off piece of rib in the lung was not a desirable thing.

Tom was all right. But like Sam, he would be a-bed for a time. Matt brought him up to date on the previous night's shooting and promised to help out around the office . . . should they need his services.

The townspeople were making plans to return to a single-store plan now that John and Bull were no longer at war, and merchandise was being moved back and forth across the street.

Matt was sitting on the bench outside the marshal's office when Van nudged him with an elbow. "Things are about to get busy around here."

Matt looked. Ross Sutton and Johnny Carlin were riding in, half a dozen mangy-looking no-counts riding in behind them. They reined up in front of the Red Dog and swung down. After being certain that

244

everyone on the streets saw them, they stomped into the saloon.

"Now what do you suppose that's all about?" Van asked, as Parley and Nate stepped out to take a look.

"I don't know," Nate replied. "But as far I know, there are no warrants out on any of them. I don't even know any of those hombres with the boys."

Doc Blaine strolled up. "Trouble coming?"

"Maybe," Matt said.

"I'd better go get my bag. Tom and Sam spent an uncomfortable night. The first night usually is. They're sleeping now. I'd hate for gunshots to wake them." He shook his head. "But I suppose until this craziness is resolved, gunshots are going to be common around here." He turned and walked back up to his office.

"Singer's standing in his door," Parley remarked.

One of the area's farmers came rattling into town, his wife on the wagon seat beside him, his kids in the bed. They pulled up in front of the general store.

"The Kendrick family," Van said. "Nice people. He keeps the hotel supplied with pork."

Ross Sutton stepped out of the saloon and hollered across the street, "You there! Kendrick! I'm talkin' to you. You keep your damn hogs penned up and off my land. I'll kill the next hog I find on my property."

Kendrick faced the young man, the street separating them. "I don't know what you're talking about, Ross. My hogs don't ever get out of the pen."

"Are you callin' me a liar, you goddamn stinkin' pig farmer?" Ross screamed.

"No," Kendrick said. "I'm saying that I don't

know what you're talking about."

"Get a gun!" Ross hollered.

Van stood up. "That's all, Sutton. Back off," he called to the man a block away. "Go on in the store, Kendrick."

"You go to hell, Dixon," Ross shouted. "I don't take orders from the likes of you."

The farmer turned and Ross pulled and shot him in the back. Kendrick pitched forward and crashed through the plate glass window of the general store.

Kendrick's oldest boy ran out of the store just as Johnny Carlin stepped out of the saloon. "Hell," Carlin said. "Might as well make it a pair." He pulled iron and shot the boy through the head. The boy fell forward and died on the boardwalk.

Matt and the deputies were running up the street. They all dived for cover as Sutton, Carlin, and their friends turned on them and opened fire. Women and kids were screaming and running for the protection of buildings and men were scrambling for guns.

Johnny Carlin coolly took aim and shot Parley just as he was diving for cover. The slug slammed into his leg and broke it just above the knee.

Ross Sutton put a .45 slug into Nate Perry's shoulder and knocked the deputy down, then both Sutton and Carlin turned their guns on Matt. Matt rolled behind a water trough as the air was filled with lead.

Lawyer Sprague grabbed up his rifle and opened fire from his office window, killing one of those with the rancher's boys. Matt came up on one knee just as the killers jumped on their horses and took off down the alley between Singer's land office and the Red Dog. He leveled his .44 and emptied a saddle before the gang disappeared. The killer tumbled from the saddle and fell under the hooves of his horse.

"Posse!" Van shouted. "To your horses, men. Matt, look after things in town."

The deputy was off at a trot, as men poured out of stores, running for their horses. Doc Blaine was running up the boardwalk, black bag in hand. The undertaker and helper were walking swiftly toward the dead and dying.

In the small clinic, Sam and Tom were awake and looking at one another, each wondering what in the hell was going on now. But they could do little else, for in order to insure they would stay in bed, Doc Blaine had hidden their clothes, leaving them clad only in short drawers that were somewhat less than modest.

Doc Blaine looked over the moaning and bloody Parley at Matt. "This tears it now," the doctor said. "Now there will be no stopping Bull or John."

"Maybe it's time," Matt said, thinking: Maybe it's past time.

8

8

Matt sent a young man on the gallop for Bull and John, and then turned his attention to the safety of the town. He did not know if the shooting was spur-of-the-monent, or whether there had been a more sinister plan behind it. He had to assume the latter and get ready for anything.

After quickly consulting with Tom Riley—and telling Sam he'd certainly seen far more appealing sights than his brother in his drawers—Matt started organizing the townspeople into a militia, posting men on rooftops and ordering all fire barrels filled in case the outlaws hit the town with the intention of burning it down. Matt just didn't have any idea what might happen next. He certainly had not anticipated the cold-blooded murder of Kendrick and his son.

That had been a totally senseless act. There was no doubt in Matt's mind that as soon as the ranchers heard the news, Bull and John would take their hands and hunt down their kids. If the fathers took their sons alive, they would hang from the nearest tree. Matt had no illusions about that. This was a hard land that demanded swift justice.

He had just finished posting the guards and securing the town as best he could against attack and fire when a thunderous rumble of hooves reached him, coming from the south end of town. He knew without looking up it was Bull and John.

The ranchers reined up and did not dismount. Matt could see that the ranchers and riders were supplied for a week on the trail and all the men packed two pistols and a rifle in a boot.

"Kendrick and his boy dead?" John asked.

"Yes."

"Our sons killed them without provocation?" Bull asked.

"Yes. Neither Kendrick or his son were armed."

"You the law in town now?" Laredo asked.

"I guess. Van's out with the posse."

"You keep the peace in town, Matt," Bull told him. "We'll send the posse back as soon as we catch up with them. This is family business."

"Bull!" Tom shouted from the door of the clinic. He stood with a blanket wrapped around him. "Both you men back off, I say."

"Sorry, Tom," John called. "This is none of your affair. We sired those kids, and I guess helped make them what they are. So it's up to us to deal with them. You just lay back down and get yourself well."

Bull and John rode slowly over to Singer's office. The man stepped out onto the boardwalk. "You be out of town when we get back, Miles," Bull told his full brother. "If you're here, I'll personally kill you and hang those gunnies you've got protecting you."

"You can't do that!" Miles screamed.

"If you're here when we get back," John told the man, "you're goin' to find out the hard way what we can and can't do. You been warned. Take heed."

Miles Singer looked over at the cowboys. He swallowed hard when he noticed the rope dangling from Laredo's saddle horn. A noose had already been fashioned. Lars carried another hangman's noose on his saddle horn.

The ranchers and their men rode out without another word. Matt loaded up two Greeners and carried them and a sack of shells up to the doctor's office, giving them to Tom and Sam. "Just in case," he said.

"I have a hunch we'll need them," Tom said. "I think the town is going to be hit."

"They're fools if they do," Matt replied.

"They have no choice, Matt," Sam spoke up. "It's an act of desperation. For men like J.B. Adams and Ben Connors and the other gunslingers, it's a matter of pride. For the kids of Bull and John . . . ?" He shook his head. "Who knows what motivates them. You just get ready. It's going to be a long afternoon and an even longer night."

At the camp of the gunslingers, J.B. Adams tossed the dredges of his coffee away and stood up. Word of Bull

Sutton and John Carlin on the prod after their kids had reached them, and the hired guns had sat down for a long talk.

"What say you, J.B.?" Paul Stewart asked.

"I'm riding into town and check in at the hotel. I'm going to have me a drink, a meal, and a hot bath. I'm going to dress in new, clean clothes, and have me a shave. Then I'm going to kill Matt Bodine."

"He is mine," Yok Zapata said, standing up as gracefully as any panther ever moved. "Raul was a friend."

"You are both wrong," Phillip Bacque said. "Matt Bodine is mine."

Big Dan Parker and Burl stood up together. Dan said, "I ain't interested in no bath and shave. But I am gonna kill Matt Bodine."

"I figure Bodine's to blame for all them good plans fallin' through," Burl said. "I aim to get lead in him."

"Well, we damn sure owe Bodine and them lousy townspeople something," Paul Mitchell said, looking at Bobby Dumas. Bobby's face was still badly burned from the scalding coffee tossed on him by the pastor's wife.

"Damn right," Bobby said.

"I owe Bodine and the town something myself," Bob Coody said, standing up. "And especially a snot-nosed, uppity little brat named Billy. I'm gonna cut that kid's ears off and hand 'em to him."

Ben Connors said nothing, he just checked both pistols and picked up his saddle, walking toward his horse.

Dick Yandle sighed and stood up, brushing himself off. He hitched at his gunbelt and picked up his saddle. He looked at Jack Norman. "You comin', Jack?"

"Oh, yeah. You, Will?"

"Count me in."

Dick Laurin and Simon Green checked their guns and walked toward their horses.

The rest of the gunfighter camp did the same. Ramblin' Ed was the last to leave. He kicked dirt over the fire and then swung into the saddle. He paused for a few seconds. "I got a bad feelin' about this, Blackie," he said to his horse. "A real bad feelin'."

He looked around and rode after the others.

Matt was tense and slightly jumpy. He went into the marshal's office and took a six-gun from a desk drawer, checking the loads and filling up the last chamber. He tucked that behind his gun belt. He moved to the gun cabinet and took down a Greener, breaking it open and loading it up with buckshot. He stuck a half dozen shells in his pocket.

Van walked in and looked at him for a moment. "What's goin' on, Matt?"

Matt turned to face the older man. "I got a bad feeling, Van. And I learned a long time ago to trust my hunches."

Van nodded his head and strapped on another gun belt. He took a rifle from the rack and checked it, adding a couple of more rounds. "Farmer John's over to the Red Dog, sittin' and drinkin' with Proctor and a couple of hard cases that drifted in about an hour ago. I don't like it. But I can't believe any bunch will try again to tree this town."

"No. I don't think that either. That dozen or so buildings south of here. Is that the original town site?"

"No. Mormons built that town about twenty years ago. Then they deserted it and other folks moved in. Changed the name to Big Ugly. Isn't that a hell of a name for a town. The second bunch didn't last long either. Nobody's lived there in ten years or so. Why?"

"I rode by there the other day. Saw smoke."

"A drifter, probably."

"How much daylight you figure we have left?"

Van looked outside. "A good six hours. It ain't a twenty minute ride down to Big Ugly. Take off if you've a mind to. Hell, Matt, every man in this town is armed and most of the women, too. I've deputized the en-tar town. It's you them hired guns is after, I'm thinking."

"You're right. But I don't want anymore gunplay in this town, Van. I'll be down in the ghost town."

"Matt, they's about twenty of them ol' boys. You don't stand a chance."

"Seventeen, I think," Matt said with an easy grin. "Maybe eighteen."

"That's close to twenty, 'way I figure it."

"I either make them come to me outside of town, or they'll come to town looking for me. And this time, some innocent people will get hurt. I don't want that on my conscience. Post guards at both ends of town. When they come looking, tell them where I am."

"No way I can talk you out of this?"

"No." Matt left the office and had the cook at the Mexican cafe fix him a couple of large sandwiches. He stopped Doc Blaine on the street and told him what he was going to do. He noticed that the doctor had once again strapped on his guns. "You give Sam a big dose of laudanum, Doc. Knock him out. All right? I don't want him to know what I'm doing."

"Very well. What you're doing is foolish, but you're right about innocent people being hurt if all those gunhands come here. We've been very lucky up to now."

"I'll see you when this is over." Matt turned to walk away.

"Matt?"

Matt stopped and looked back at the doctor.

"As you have no doubt noticed, I handle a gun pretty well. You want me to go along with you?"

"No. I don't think the whole bunch will show up." He smiled. "At least I'm hoping they won't. One against eighteen is not real great odds."

Matt stopped by the jail to pick up more shells for the Greener and took the back way out of town so he would not be seen on the main street. Sam might be watching. And even with aching and broken ribs, he would try to accompany his brother. And Tom would probably attempt to arrest Matt in order to stop him. It was only a short ride to the ghost town of Big Ugly.

He picketed his horse on good graze by a stream and, taking his rifle and shotgun and saddlebags, he walked across the meadow to the warping and rotting boards and buildings of the old town. As he walked, he could detect the very faint odor of smoke.

I've got to get that drifter out of here, Matt thought. If he hasn't already moved on.

Halfway across the meadow, he stopped and hunkered down, as a strange feeling swept over him. Something was wrong, his senses were telling him. Something was all out of whack here.

Then he heard a horse whinny.

He remained motionless in the tall grass and watched as a man came out of a building and walked to a falling down old shed. Something about the man was very familiar, but at this distance, Matt could not make out any facial features. And the big floppy hat didn't help matters any.

The man saw to his horse and returned to the shack. Matt still had no idea who it was. But he was carrying a rifle. Matt made his way to the town, staying low and using whatever cover he could find in the meadow. He stayed close to the rear of the buildings and began working his way toward the shack of the stranger.

The sounds of humming reached him. The man was relaxed, at least, suspecting nothing. Then the man began singing softly. Damn, but that voice was familiar.

Matt edged closer. He tried to look inside but the window glass was so dirty he could make out only a vague shape. But even the faint shape was familiar to him. Who was this guy? What the hell was he doing here?

Matt moved to the door and listened to the soft singing. He made up his mind. He had to do something, and time was running out for him. The hired guns would be here shortly, he felt sure. He pulled his .44 from leather and pushed open the door, stepping inside.

Matt Bodine and the man looked at each other, both of them startled, and one of them very puzzled. Both men were speechless for a few seconds.

"You!" Matt said.

The man smiled. But his eyes were anything but friendly. He was not wearing a pistol, and the rifle was leaning up against a wall, too far away for him to reach.

"In the flesh, Matt." He laughed at Matt's expression. "You'd better close your mouth before a fly decides to take up residence in there. How have you been?"

Matt closed his mouth and holstered his pistol.

"That's better," the man said, still squatting on the dirty floor.

"What the hell is going on here?"

"I've been playing a game. A fun game, isn't it?"

"Not particularly. And it's one I don't understand. Did you slip that note under my door?"

"Certainly."

"You knew all along about Sutton and Carlin and Singer and Ladue?"

"Even before I came out here. Ladue is my uncle, too."

"Jesus! How many kids did that old man sire?"

"Four. All illegitimate."

"And you have the proof of that?"

"You're very quick, Bodine. Yes."

"You're working with Ladue?"

"Wrong, Bodine," the voice came from behind him. "He's working for me."

9

Matt didn't have to turn around. The voice belonged to the old mountain man, Ladue.

"This here ol' Sharps will blow your backbone plumb out your belly, Bodine," Ladue said. "So keep your hands away from them guns."

"You better keep me alive," Matt said. "In about an hour, or less, this place will be filled up with hired guns."

"Sure, all working for us," the man still squatting on the floor said.

"You don't have that kind of money."

"They're working on speculation, Matt. For a bigger piece of the pie at the end of the road."

"That being when Sutton and Carlin are dead, and with you and Ladue laying claim to all their holdings."

"Right! Of course, we'd have to kill the wives, but that would be no problem. And the kids are already written out of the wills. Clever, right?"

Matt stood very still, saying nothing. Everything was all wrapped up now, tied with a nice, neat bow. He even had a pretty good idea what the two men had planned for him. Matt knew it all now. He had to make a play, but not with that big Sharps pointed at him. Lead from that Sharps could knock a two thousand pound buffalo down.

"Now what?" Matt asked.

Ladue moved slowly around to Matt's right side, staying out of reach. The old man was cautious, knowing Matt's reputation. "Now we wait," Ladue said.

"Wait for what?"

But Ladue would only smile.

The man on the floor said, "The gunfighters are going to start earning their keep."

"I get it," Matt said. "I get to kill as many as possible."

"By golly!" Ladue said with an evil grin. "Now you know, we never thought of that."

"I just bet you didn't," Matt's reply was dry. His eyes touched the rifle leaning against the wall. "Gates' rifle. You hired him and then you killed him, right?"

"No," Ladue said. "We didn't hire him, and we didn't kill him."

"The Carlin and Sutton girls hired him to kill their brothers," the man on the floor said. "Nice kids, aren't they?"

"How do you know all that?"

"Johnny Carlin told J.B. Adams that and J.B. told us," Ladue said.

260

"Who killed him?"

"Bacque."

"On orders from the kids?"

"No. It was personal. They didn't like each other."

"What do you plan to do with Singer?"

The man on the floor smiled. "Those bodyguards he hired are working for us. That answer your question?"

"A few things still puzzle me."

"Ask."

Matt looked at the man on the floor. "How are you going to claim any part of the estate?"

"From a long distance away. Like New York City."

"So you stay . . . ?"

"Gone and forgotten."

"Slick. I'll give you that much. Very slick. When does Singer get a bullet?"

"All in good time."

"You mind if I roll a smoke?"

"Go right ahead," Ladue told him. "It might be your last one."

Matt slowly rolled and licked and lit. Neither man seemed to notice as he dropped the still burning match to the floor, in the middle of a pile of trash and paper. Within seconds, flames shot up.

Startled, Ladue shifted his eyes to the leaping flames just for an instant. Matt shot him, the slug doubling the man over. Just to be on the safe side, knowing how tough old mountain men were, Matt shot him again, then shifted the muzzle to the man scrambling frantically on his hands and knees across the dirty floor for Gates' rifle. Matt plugged him twice, kicked the rifle out of the way, and stomped out the fire.

He checked on Ladue, and the man was cold dead. Then he knelt down beside the still-alive and new-found brother to Singer, Sutton, and Carlin.

"You don't have long," he told the man. "If you have anything to say, you better get it said."

"You still lose," the man gasped. "The gunfighters are on their way. They'll kill you."

"No, they won't. Who would pay them?"

Some of the light seemed to leave the man's eyes. He shook his head slowly. "You never did suspect me, though, did you?"

"Of keeping things stirred up, yes. Of being a brother, no."

"Why in the hell did you have to come along, Bodine?"

"Just lucky, I guess."

The man's eyes rolled back, his head lolled to one side, and he slumped full length and dead to the dirty floor.

Matt was waiting for the gunfighters when they rode into the ghost town. He held up one hand.

"It's over, boys," he told them. "You know that Bull and John won't rest until their debt is paid with their kids. Your employers, Ladue and his partner, are dead. In that shack. You want to take a look, help yourselves."

J.B. Adams and Ben Connors swung down and looked. Both men grunted. They walked back to the horses and mounted up, Ben saying, "I don't hire my guns for free, boys. The paymasters are dead. You want to shoot it out with Bodine for free, you go right ahead, but you're damn fools if you do." He and J.B. rode off without another look back.

Slowly, the others followed. In a matter of only a few seconds, Matt Bodine stood alone in the weedy street of the old Idaho ghost town called Big Ugly. He fetched his horse and his saddlebags and sat on the boardwalk under part of an awning and ate his sandwiches, drinking coffee he'd found in the shack.

The gunfighters had headed back toward town, most of them hanging their guns on the saddlehorn to show they were peaceful and were provisioning up and moving on. Those that still held hostile feelings toward the townspeople would head elsewhere. It wouldn't be long before someone would ride out to check on Matt.

Just about an hour before dusk, Doc Blaine and several other townspeople and a couple of the smaller ranch owners rode out.

"J.B. Adams says it's over," Doc Blaine said. "At least as far as he's concerned. He and about six more rode east. J.B., Ben Connors, Dick Yandle, Burl Golden, and a few I didn't know. They said there would always be another day. The others are camped outside of town. I don't know what they're up to."

"Bull and John?" Matt asked.

"They can't find their kids. But they did tangle with the scum the kids had hired. Van put those that survived the shootout in jail. They're right behind us."

"No idea where the kids are?"

"No. Bull thinks they've left the country. I hope so.

I hope they never come back."

"Singer?"

"He's alone now. His bodyguards left with J.B. and the others. That is one frightened man, Matt. He's sure that either Bull or John will kill him."

"I'm not. Although one or the other might give him a good butt-whipping."

"So it's over, now?" a rancher asked.

Matt shook his head. "No. Not with the Carlin and Sutton kids still out there full of hate, and those gunslicks still hanging around. It isn't over. But it's getting there."

Matt had built a small fire and had moved the coffee pot from the shack outside. He had rounded up several cups, although many Western men carried a battered tin cup with them.

"Coffee's fresh and hot," Matt said. "Help yourselves." He looked up as hoofbeats sounded. John Carlin and Bull Sutton rode into the old ghost town, several of their hands with them.

"This was a crazy stunt, boy!" Bull said, stepping down. "You against seventeen or eighteen gunslicks. I ought to take a belt to your backside." He grinned. "But I'm afraid you might take it away from me and use it on my own butt."

A few weeks back, the man would not have been a big enough person to have said the latter.

"Of course, you would certainly richly deserve that," John kidded him, and both men laughed. They were growing closer each day.

Van Dixon rode up and swung down. He was the first to notice Wilbur Gates' fancy rifle leaning up against one of the remaining awning support posts. "Where'd you get that, Matt?"

Matt jerked his thumb toward the shack. "Off of the mastermind of this whole sorry, bloody mess."

Doc Blaine, Van Dixon, Bull, and John, stepped carefully up on the rotting boards, and Blaine pushed open the warped door. The men looked in, looked back at Matt, and shook their heads. Doc closed the door, and the men walked back to the fire and the coffee pot, for with the gathering of shadows, the air was growing cool. No one spoke until those who wanted coffee had their cups filled and were sitting or squatting around the fire.

"I don't know the whole story, but they told me a lot of it," Matt said. He then told the men everything he had learned at gunpoint in the cabin.

"So there were four brothers," Van was the first to speak. "But who was the man we buried?"

"Some drifter, probably," Matt said. "For sure, we'll never know."

"Did those two in yonder have a hand in turning our kids against us?" John asked.

Matt shook his head. "I can't answer that, John. I just don't know. You'll probably never know. Not unless your kids have a change of heart and level with you."

Bull snorted. "Not much chance of that happening, Matt. The girls are gone. All of them except Connie. And I say good riddance." The rancher did not volunteer any information as to where the girls had gone, and Matt did not ask.

The men drank their coffee and stowed away the

cups. Matt carefully put out the fire. "Somebody round up the horses of the dead men," John said. "We'll tie them across their saddles and head on back."

The men carried out Ladue and put him belly down across his saddle and tied him down snug. Then the body of Ralph Masters, editor and owner of *The Express* was carried out and tossed across the saddle and his hands tied firmly to his feet under the horse's belly.

"He shot that drifter in the face with a shotgun?" Van asked, looking at the body of the newspaper man.

"I guess so," Matt said. "I never got a chance to ask them. Or maybe Ladue killed him. They probably gave the man some of Ralph's clothing—clothes that all the townspeople had seen him wearing many times—and then killed him."

"But why did they kill the poor sot?" Bull asked. "That wasn't necessary. Their plan would have worked without killing some drifter."

Matt shook his head. "I don't know all the answers, Bull. I wish I did. Maybe they were running scared. When Sam and I started sticking our noses into the trouble, we certainly stirred up a hornet's nest. Ralph asked me why in the hell we had to come along."

"What'd you tell him?" Van asked.

"I said we were just lucky, I guess."

All the men stood for a moment and looked at the lashed-down bodies. John finally broke the silence. "Lucky for us. Masters' luck just ran out."

10

The citizens of Crossville lined the streetlamp-lit boardwalks as the men rode in single file. They were all, men and women, heavily armed, and they stood silent as the men reined in and swung down. The undertaker and his helper removed the bodies and toted them off.

"Matt?" Bull spoke softly in the night. "You don't think it's over, do you?"

"No. J.B. and Ben and a few like him, well, this is a job of work. Nothing personal. Men like Yok and Phillip Bacque and Ramblin' Ed, this cuts against the grain. They've got to call me out to save face. But it won't be here. I'm going to stock up in the morning and head on back down to Big Ugly. I'll wait for them there."

"You'll have men with you, Matt," Doc Blaine spoke over the saddle of Matt's horse. "That's firm, and we'll brook no arguments on the matter."

"Who do you have in mind?" Matt asked, thinking

that he already knew the answer.

Bull said, "Me. John. And Doc Blaine. And in case you didn't know—and I'm sure you don't, only a few of us do—Doc Blaine was one of Mosby's Raiders during the War Between the States."

The doctor was clearly startled. "How in the hell did you find that out?"

The rancher smiled. "I snooped around, sawbones. Me and John will send word back to the wives that we're stayin' in town. We'll provision up in the morning and head out. That suit you, Doc?"

"I'll be ready."

"I'm going to see Sam and bring him up to date, then I'll meet you all over at the hotel for a steak," Matt said.

"See you in a few minutes."

"I wish I was going with you," Sam said, when Matt told him of his plans.

"I wish you were, too. When this is over, Sam, let's you and me think about heading back home and settling down."

"I think it's time, brother. Of course, that is no guarantee that we'll stay there twelve months out of the year."

Matt laughed, and he and Sam shot the breeze instead of other people for a few minutes. Doc Blaine's nurse came in and shooed Matt out, giving him just enough time to say hello to Tom, who had just awakened.

"Sam will fill you in, Tom," Matt told him. "This mess is just about over."

"Suits the hell out of me," Tom said, then yawned.

An hour later, his belly full of steak and potatoes and apple pie, Matt rolled into bed and didn't wake up until five the next morning, with Bull Sutton hammering on the hotel room door.

After breakfast, the men provisioned and headed out to the old town of Big Ugly. They rode heavily armed and with their jaws set in determination. Bull and John knew well that their sons might show up with the gunfighters. Both men had resigned themselves to that.

Both John and Bull had left word for Miles Singer. Should he be in town when they got back, they would hang him. Miles went panting and flapping to the wounded Tom Riley.

"If they don't hang you," Tom told him, "I will."

Singer was packed and gone by eight o'clock that morning. Shortly before ten o'clock, Paul Stewart, Simon Green, Dick Laurin, and a gunfighter called Buck came riding into town.

"They're waiting for you down at the ghost town," Van told the quartet. "You know where Big Ugly is?"

"We know," Paul said.

"We'll have us a beer and wait for our friends," Buck said.

"Yeuh," Van drawled. "I figured you'd all have to ride down there in a bunch."

The gunhands had noticed on their way in that everybody in town was armed—heavily. They turned their backs to Van and entered the Red Dog.

Les King, Willie Durham, Farmer John, and Sam

Hawkins came in a few minutes later.

Van pointed them to the saloon. "Your mouth broke?" Les King asked the deputy.

"No. And neither is this sawed-off ten-gauge," Van told him. "Now shut your goddamn trap, punk. And carry it over there to the saloon and fill it full of rotgut courage so's you can face real men."

None of the four liked that, but they offered no rebuttal.

Ned Kerry, Paul Brown, and Big Dan Parker came in next.

Van pointed to the saloon.

Bob Coody, Ramblin' Ed Clark, and Bill Lowry were the next to come riding in. They didn't have to ask directions. They reined up and walked into the saloon.

Jennings, Norman, and Chuck came in, followed by Yok Zapata and Phillip Bacque. Proctor came in alone, followed by Donner, Nyeburn, Chase Martin, and Blue Anderson.

"Twenty-four," Sam said from his bed by the window. "And if the Sutton-Carlin brood throws in with that bunch, that'll make it thirty-one to four. That, Tom, is pretty crappy odds."

"I can drive a buggy with one hand if you can stand the ride," Tom offered.

"I know where our clothes are hidden. All freshly laundered, too."

"What are we waiting for?"

"You're not leavin' me out of this," Nate Perry yelled from behind the partition. "My gun arm ain't busted."

"All right, Nate. Get out of bed and come on."

"Get my leg out of this harness!" Parley hollered. "I'm goin', too."

"No way, boy," Tom told him. "You stay here in case Van needs some help. We'll roll your bed by this window and leave you a rifle."

A young boy walked by the clinic, and Tom tapped on the window glass, startling the lad. "Eddie, you go down to the livery and tell Ron I said to hitch us up a two-seater buggy, fill the back end with hay, and bring it behind the clinic. Quickly. Move, boy!"

"Bobby Dumas and Paul Mitchell ridin' in," Nate said. "Old ghost town is gonna be crowded."

Doc Blaine had taped Sam's ribs tight, so as long as he didn't make any sudden moves, he was relatively free of pain.

The wounded deputies hobbled, gimped, and limped out to the rear of Blaine's office, while the nurse hollered and squalled at them, threatening dire consequences, and got into the buggy, Sam in the hay-filled back. Tom clucked at the horses, and they headed for Big Ugly.

The gunhands, gathered at the Red Dog and bellied up to the bar, did not see their departure.

At the ghost town, the men made ready.

"No telling how many they'll be," Matt said. "So we'd better play this by ear. As outnumbered as we'll be, this is not going to be face to face and draw. I can't imagine the gunhands even thinking it will be. We've all stashed spare pistols in the buildings. So just as soon as we see them coming, we'll head for our spots and let them open the ball."

"Who the hell is that comin'?" John asked.

"It's a buggy," Bull said.

"Something tells me I know who it is," Doc Blaine said.

"You crazy fools!" Bull yelled, as the buggy came to a halt.

"Howdy, boys," Tom said. "Matt, you hide the buggy and team with your horses, and the rest of you help us down from here and get us into place. I don't think we've got much time."

"Twenty-six the last count," Sam said, as Matt helped him down from the hay-filled rear of the buggy. "No sign of any of your kids," Sam added, looking at the ranchers.

"They'll be along," Bull said grimly. "You can bet they've had somebody watching the town."

"Let's get set," Tom suggested.

At the extreme south end of the town was what used to be the dry goods store. Sam was placed there. Bull took the saloon. John chose the old falling down bank building. Tom was placed in the old saddle shop, almost directly across from Sam. Nate took a building catty-cornered from the bank. Blaine chose the old apothecary shop.

"And you, Matt?" Bull questioned.

"I'm going to wander. I think I can be more effective that way. But I'll stay on the west side of town to avoid any confusion. As long as I can," he added.

The men shook hands and took up positions.

The sons of John Carlin and Bull Sutton and those few ne'er-do-wells who rode with them, met the gang of gunfighters about midway between Crossville and Big Ugly. Hugh Sutton said, "You might have to wait a few months for your money," he told the hired guns, "but I'll pay you all handsomely for the deaths of Bull and John."

"Sounds good to me," Farmer John said. "Let's ride."

"Here they come!" Matt shouted from the loft of the old livery stable at the north end of town. "I'd guess a good thirty-five of them."

"Any of our kids with them?" John shouted, being closest to Matt's temporary location.

"I think so, Bull! Yes! I can make out Johnny and Hugh."

"Sorry, selfish, greedy little crap-heads," John muttered, and jacked back the hammers to his guns.

The gang reined up several hundred yards from the silent old town.

"They're waitin' in ambush," Ramblin' Ed Clark said, after a moment's staring at the town. "We go ridin' in there hell bent for leather, and they'll blow half of us out of the saddle first thing."

"Stash the horses and go in on foot," Phillip Bacque said, dismounting. "Take your rifles and stuff your pockets with cartridges."

"Split up into four groups about the same size," Simon Green suggested. "We'll start workin' our way around the town and at my yell, we'll attack."

"Hell, there ain't but four of them," Ross Sutton said, disgust in his voice. "Let's just ride and shoot it out. It won't take long."

"Go ahead," Yok Zapata said, glancing at the

young man. "That way we can see where the men are waiting in ambush. We will say nice words over your grave."

Ross didn't think much of that idea at all. He shut his mouth and kept it closed.

In the ghost town, the men waited patiently. They all knew that if they kept their heads about them and didn't jump the gun, they could cut the odds down by a full one-fourth at the first volley.

The outlaws, gunfighters, and disgruntled sons fanned out, slowly circling the town. The seven in the town waited. A few of the seven could have dropped some of those stalking them. But they waited until more showed themselves. In the distance, a horse whinnied and stamped its foot. Birds sang and soared in the sky.

Blue Anderson stepped into the rear of the old apothecary shop, and Doc Blaine had no choice in the matter. He turned and filled the hired gun's belly full of his own special prescription for outlawism. Blue staggered out the space where the door used to be and fell to the ground, his guns falling from his fingers and his eyes wide and staring at the sky. Doc waited.

Before the echo of the shot had faded, Matt drilled a man through the brisket and set him on the ground on his butt, hollering in pain.

John Carlin lifted his Greener and blew a hole in Proctor big enough to stick a telegraph pole through. Proctor was lifted off his boots by the hideous killing blast and was dead before he hit the ground.

Sam Hawkins jumped into the dusty, cobwebby

saddle shop and peered into the murk, his eyes not adjusting from the bright light outside.

"You looking for someone special?" Tom said.

Hawkins spun around, and Tom gave him two .45 rounds, one in the belly and the other in the chest. Hawkins did a little dance step to the tune of his guns falling and rattling to the floor, and then he followed them down into the dust. He drummed his boots on the floor in a final exit and then lay still.

Marcel Carlin jumped into the old dry goods store and spotted Sam Two Wolves. "Goddamn breed!" he yelled, and started blasting away in the gloom. He didn't hit a thing. Sam coolly turned and leveled a .44 and drilled the young man in the shoulder, the slug breaking the shoulder and knocking the youngest Carlin outside. He lost one gun when he hit the ground, and crawled away, blubbering and cussing.

Paul Stewart took a chance and tried to run across the weedy street, both pistols blazing and blasting. Four pistols barked. The hired gun danced and jerked his way into death and collapsed in the dirt. His guns went off as he hit the ground, sending up a shower of dirt and pebbles.

Marcel crawled across the alleyway and under the building occupied by Nate. Nate heard the scratching and waited, staring down through a hole in the rotting floor. Marcel stuck a gun up through the hole, and Nate blew the gun out of the young man's hand, taking a couple of fingers with the smashed pistol. Marcel hollered and shrieked and scurried like a big rat out from under the building. He crawled out behind a dilapidated old outhouse and wrapped a

275

handkerchief around his ruined right hand. He wished he'd never listened to his brothers. He wished he was back home. He wished he'd never plotted and schemed to kill his mother and father. He heard a buzzing and froze in horror. Then he felt the hot lash of fangs. He screamed and lifted his left hand. A big rattler was holding onto the fleshy part of his hand, the fangs somehow caught. Marcel jumped up and went running and screaming across the meadow toward his horse, his heart pumping wildly. He made about two hundred yards before he collapsed face down amid the wild flowers. He shrieked and wailed but no one heard him over the roar of gunfire. It took him a few minutes to die. They were not pleasant moments. But Marcel had never been a very pleasant young man. The huge rattler, as big around as an average man's forearm, bit Marcel a few more times in the face, just for good measure. Marcel had fallen on the snake's tail. Pissed the rattler off something fierce.

"You damn greasy Injun!" Nyeburn roared, locating Sam's position and vividly remembering the thorough butt-whipping Sam had laid on him inside and outside of Singer's office. "I'll kill you."

He came running toward the old store from the south side, ducking and dodging and running from tree to bush. Sam waited. Nyeburn stepped in a hole and went sprawling, losing both guns and bashing his head against a stump, knocking himself unconscious and putting himself out for the duration.

"Idiot," Sam muttered, and leaned against the wall, waiting, trying to forget the ache in his ribs.

"Give this up, boys!" Tom Riley yelled.

"Hell with you," Johnny Carlin returned the yell. "You're all gonna die right here. You hear me, Big John. I'm tired of livin' in your shadow. I'm gonna be known as the man who killed Big John Carlin. Me, you son of a bitch."

"Well, you got part of it right, boy," Big John Carlin said. He leveled his .45 and shot his oldest son through the belly. The father fought back tears.

11

"Johnny!" Clement screamed. "That was Pa who shot you. Pa did. Goddamn you, Big John."

"Oh, my God," Bull muttered. "Dear God, help us all for the mistakes we've made with our kids."

"Bull!" Big Dan Parker bellered.

Bull said nothing. He waited.

"How much is your life worth, Bull?" Parker yelled. "Sign your ranch over to us, Bull, and you can ride out."

"You have to be kidding," Bull muttered. He thought he knew where the voice was coming from. He holstered his pistol and picked up his Winchester, earing back the hammer.

"You hear me, John!" Parker yelled. "Take your wife and your yeller boy and ride out."

Bull put four rounds as fast as he could lever into the side of the old building. Seconds passed in silence. Big Dan Parker came staggering out, the front of his shirt, from neck to waist, was bloody. He swayed for a moment, then fell on his face in the dirt and weeds.

"Damn you all to the fires of Hell!" Paul Brown yelled. "Me and Dan was buddies." He jumped out into the street and tried to race across it.

He didn't make it. The hail of bullets turned him around and around and dropped him dead, not more than three feet from his buddy.

Two of those would-be toughs who came in with the Sutton-Carlin kids made it back to their horses and lit a shuck out, heading for safer places.

"Cowards!" Hugh Sutton hollered, half-rising from behind a water barrel. Nate sighted him in and knocked him sprawling. He got up, and Bull drilled him clean. Hugh fell to the ground and did not move.

"Damn you!" Randy screamed. "Damn you, Bull." He emptied both pistols at the old saloon building, hitting nothing but warped and rotting boards. He pulled two more pistols out from behind his belt, and Doc Blaine sighted him in and blew one of his knees into pebbles. The young man screamed in pain and passed out on the boardwalk.

"Insanity," Bull muttered.

From the loft of the livery, Matt had been watching Yok Zapata inch his way behind the buildings on the east side of the old town. Not being a man who was terribly interested in fair play with someone who was trying very hard to kill him in any way possible, Matt lifted the .44-.40 he'd taken from Ralph Masters and plugged the half-Apache from four hundred yards away. Yok stumbled around for a moment, and then, purely unintentionally, sat down in an old wooden chair and looked at the hole in his chest.

"Well, I'll just be damned!" Yok said, and died, his chin on his chest.

"Yok!" Bacque shouted. "Where are you, Yok?"

"Dead," Ned Kerry called in a hoarse whisper. "He got drilled from someone in the livery over yonder. In the loft."

"Then that man is dead," the French-Canadian vowed, and began slipping around to the edge of the last building on that side of the street. "Whoever he might be."

"Bodine, I think," Ned said.

"All the better," Bacque replied.

Matt watched his progress carefully, but he could get no clear shot. Bacque was being very cautious. Matt heard a noise on the floor below him and with a silent curse, left the opening and moved silently to the ladder. He looked down just as Simon Green looked up.

Matt shot him with the .44-.40 at a distance of about twenty feet, the slug striking the gunhand in the center of the forehead. Simon had hired his gun out for the last time.

Matt heard boots on the floor before him and figured it was Bacque. He moved silently to stand on several bales of old hay and was just in time, for Bacque started filling the old barn loft floor with bullet holes. Several hit the tightly bound bales but did not penetrate.

"Come on down and fight me, Bodine," Bacque called.

Matt said nothing.

"You want me to come up, hey? Well, my mother raised no fools, Bodine."

Matt waited, listening to him reload both pistols. He closed the loading gate with a faint snap.

"I will let you safely down the ladder, Bodine."

Sure you will, Matt thought. Of course, you're such a gentleman.

Bacque started filling the loft floor with holes. Matt kicked a bale of hay over, and it landed with a thump. He removed a spur and groaned loudly, then tossed the spur to the floor. It rattled once, and the big barn was still and warm in the sun.

"If it is a trick, it is a very convincing one, Bodine," Bacque called.

Matt saw the ladder tremble under the gunfighter's weight. He raised the already cocked rifle.

Bacque's hat appeared, then the man chuckled. "I am glad you are dead, Bodine. I just bought that hat. Had you fallen for the hat-on-a-stick trick I would be very angry."

His head appeared, and Matt shot him in the center of the face. Bacque tumbled to the lower floor. Matt did not have to look to see if he was dead. A .44-.40 slug in the face at about ten feet doesn't leave much room for doubt. He was walking back to his post when he heard the rumble of many horses at a full gallop.

"Riders comin'!" a gunfighter shouted.

"Jesus Christ!" another shouted. "Must be a hundred of them."

"Ring the town," Matt heard Lars call. "No one gets out alive unless they want to surrender."

Pistols and rifles started hitting the ground, and men began leaving their positions and walking out into the street, their hands held high.

"All right, all right!" Ramblin' Ed called. "We yield. It's over."

"I'll be goddamned if we do," came another shout, and Ross Sutton and Clement and Pete Carlin ran out into the street, screaming curses and guns blazing at the posse members. John and Bull lifted their rifles. The men had tears in their eyes as they opened fire.

Matt averted his eyes as the fathers cut down their outlaw sons.

It was over.

12

Johnny Carlin and Randy Sutton lived through the fight. Randy's leg was amputated at the knee, and Johnny would spend months recovering from his stomach wound. Randy eventually went to college and after that became a traveling tent preacher. Johnny drank himself to death. Marcel, Clement, and Pete Carlin, and Hugh and Ross Sutton were buried in the old cemetery of the ghost town, along with the bodies of the slain gunmen.

Doc Blaine hung up his guns.

Daniel Carlin and Connie Sutton were married shortly after the fight at Big Ugly.

Nyeburn recovered from his head wound and was sentenced to a prison term, along with the other hired guns. All of the hired guns vowed someday to kill Matt Bodine and Sam Two Wolves.

The daughters of Bull Sutton and John Carlin were never heard from again. If Petunia made it as an actress, she did it under a different name.

Tom Riley was elected sheriff of the county, and Nate Perry was elected marshal of Crossville.

Parley Davis became a full-time deputy sheriff.

Van Dixon married Miss Charlotte.

Miles Singer left town and dropped out of sight.

John and Ginny and Bull and Roz adopted a whole orphanage of kids and proceeded to start life anew.

Matt Bodine and Sam Two Wolves . . .

"You look healthy enough to me," Matt said to Sam.

"I am healthy enough to throw you in the creek."

"Don't try it," Matt warned with a grin. "I'd hate to put you back in the hospital."

The brothers were tying their bedrolls behind the cantles of their saddles.

"Where to this time?" Sam asked.

"Well, I believe we discussed going home."

"I didn't think you took that very seriously."

Matt's grin widened.

"That's what I thought."

Lawyer Sprague walked up. "Well, boys. What trail do you take now?"

"We were just talking about that," Matt said.

"And . . . ?"

"I guess we'll know when we get to the crossroads," Sam said.

"You've got to settle down someday," the lawyer said.

The blood brothers nodded in agreement, swung into the saddle, and both of them lifted a hand in farewell. They pointed the noses of their horses west and slowly rode out of town.

Little Billy, his dog by his side, waved at the brothers.

Matt and Sam returned the wave, Matt saying, "That makes it all worth it."

"You are a hopeless romantic," Sam said. "But I suppose I shall have to tag along, watching you endlessly tilt at windmills."

"You're a pretty good tilter yourself," Matt said.

The brothers grinned at each other and rode on to write another page of Western history.